"You're a g[...]

With a kind heart. I'm sure I won't be the only woman in Royal who appreciates your sterling qualities."

"Aw, hell. You're making fun of me, aren't you?"

"Maybe a little." She smiled gently. "Six months ago your virtue might have been in danger. But now I have three babies to consider. Their welfare has to come before anything else in my life."

"Even romance?"

"Especially romance."

"Then I guess we've cleared the air."

"I guess we have."

"I should go," he said. But he didn't move.

Simone stood up, swaying a bit before she steadied herself with a hand on the back of the chair. "Yes, you should."

Squaring his shoulders, he nodded. The urge to kiss her was overpowering.

She kept a hand on the chair, either because she felt faint or because she intended to use it as a shield. Either way, it didn't matter. He wanted to taste her more than he wanted his next breath.

* * *

Triplets for the Texan is part of the series
Texas Cattleman's Club: Blackmail—

No secret—or heart—is safe in Royal, Texas...

Dear Reader,

I think it's safe to say that lots of people make crazy mistakes or dumb decisions in their late teens and early twenties. Hopefully, most of those ill-conceived "stumbles" remain anonymous, or at the very least don't have lasting consequences.

My heroine, Simone, has a good heart, but she's impulsive. She's already lost a man she cares about, and now her own grandfather has died and left behind a will Simone finds hurtful and insulting. In the midst of her righteous indignation, she heads down a road that has serious consequences. By the time she struggles with second thoughts, it's too late. She's pregnant!

I hope you enjoy Simone's story. I think you'll fall for Hutch and wonder how she ever let him get away the first time.

Welcome back to Royal, Texas, and the tales of the Texas Cattleman's Club.

Happy Reading,

Janice Maynard

JANICE MAYNARD

—

TRIPLETS FOR THE TEXAN

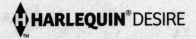

Special thanks and acknowledgment are given to Janice Maynard for her contribution to the Texas Cattleman's Club: Blackmail series.

Recycling programs
for this product may
not exist in your area.

ISBN-13: 978-0-373-83843-1

Triplets for the Texan

HARLEQUIN®
www.Harlequin.com

Printed in U.S.A.

USA TODAY bestselling author **Janice Maynard** loved books and writing even as a child. But it took multiple rejections before she sold her first manuscript. Since 2002, she has written over forty-five books and novellas. Janice lives in east Tennessee with her husband, Charles. They love hiking, traveling and spending time with family.

You can connect with Janice at janicemaynard.com, Twitter.com/janicemaynard, Facebook.com/janicemaynardreaderpage, Facebook.com/janicesmaynard and Instagram.com/janicemaynard.

Books by Janice Maynard

Harlequin Desire

Texas Cattleman's Club: Blackmail

Triplets for the Texan

The Kavanaghs of Silver Glen

A Not-So-Innocent Seduction
Baby for Keeps
Christmas in the Billionaire's Bed
Twins on the Way
Second Chance with the Billionaire
How to Sleep with the Boss
For Baby's Sake

The Men of Wolff Mountain

Into His Private Domain
A Touch of Persuasion
Impossible to Resist
The Maid's Daughter
All Grown Up
Taming the Lone Wolff
A Wolff at Heart

Visit her Author Profile page at Harlequin.com, or janicemaynard.com, for more titles.

For Charles Griemsman, editor extraordinaire.
Thanks for all your hard work and
your commitment to making stories shine.
The Texas Cattleman's Club wouldn't be
the same without you!

One

Royal, Texas, was a great place to call home. Running her own ad agency, being a member of the esteemed Texas Cattleman's Club and maintaining a hectic social life kept Simone Parker plenty busy. Busy enough not to worry about the ghosts of lost loves.

Today, her luck had run out. Five years. It had been five long years since she'd last laid eyes on Troy Hutchinson. Now here she sat in a freezing exam room at Royal Memorial, naked but for a thin paper hospital gown, and in walked the man who broke her heart. Pressing her knees together instinctively, she gripped the edge of the exam table and blurted out the first thing that came to her mind.

"Where's Dr. Markman?"

Hutch—almost nobody called him Troy—stared at her impassively. "He took a position in Houston.

I'm the new head of the maternal-fetal medicine department."

Made sense. Royal's state-of-the-art hospital hired only the best.

It occurred to her that Hutch didn't look at all surprised to see her. But then again, he'd obviously glanced at her chart before entering the room. He was as gorgeous as ever—chocolate eyes, closely cropped black hair and mocha skin. The only thing missing was his killer smile.

Tall and lean, in his physical prime, the man was impressive even without the lab coat. Wearing it, he exuded authority and masculinity. Making Simone feel small and stupid.

Her stomach curled with nausea. Today's situation was volatile enough without having to confront old lovers. As if the term applied. She'd been a twenty-two-year-old virgin when she and Hutch first hooked up. She'd had only one relationship after that, and it had been brief and unexceptional.

For most of her life she'd chosen to hide behind her reputation as a shallow party girl. Even Hutch had believed it in the beginning. Until he'd realized he was the first. Then there had been hell to pay.

Her palms started to sweat. "You can't be my doctor."

"Of course not," he said. "Dr. Markman left rather abruptly. We've been in the process of notifying his patients. Somehow, your appointment fell through the cracks. Dr. Janine Fetter has agreed to take over your case…with your permission, of course."

"That's fine," Simone said impatiently. "But that doesn't explain why *you're* here."

A faint smile lightened his face. "Don't shoot the messenger. Scheduling should have postponed your ultrasound until next week. Dr. Fetter doesn't have any openings until then. She's not even here today."

Great, just great. Hutch knew every inch of her body. Even so, no way in heck was she going to calmly put her feet in those stirrups and let him examine her. That was too icky for words. "What are my options?"

"You can make an appointment for next week and go home…"

"Or?"

"Or if you don't want to wait, I can go over the ultrasound with you. But no exam," he said quickly.

"Ah." Simone had badgered the tech to explain all the grainy images on the screen, but the woman had been well trained. She'd done her job, escorted Simone to yet another exam room and left her to worry for forty-five minutes. Plenty of time for a single woman to regret the impulsive decision that had led her to this moment.

"So tell me," she snapped, her nerves getting the best of her. "I'm not pregnant, am I? Don't worry. I won't fall apart. I knew the odds when I went into this."

Pursuing fertility treatments and intrauterine insemination had been more involved than she had ever imagined. Even now, she wouldn't be entirely unhappy if it hadn't worked. Picking out a sperm donor and dealing with hormone shots had been stressful, expensive and time-consuming. It had also given her plenty of opportunity to rethink her hasty decision.

Her late grandfather had left instructions with the executors of his will that she would be entitled to half of his vast estate—five million dollars cash and the family homestead, worth infinitely more—if, and only if, she produced an heir to continue the family bloodline. With no plans to settle down anytime soon, she'd decided to go the route of single motherhood.

Trying to live up to the terms of her grandfather's will—without weighing the cost—was, in retrospect, probably a stupid decision.

She must have had gut-level doubts from the beginning, because she hadn't even told her two best friends, Naomi and Cecelia. Naomi had seemed distracted and tense ever since she got back from Europe, and Cecelia had been on cloud nine after reuniting with former flame Deacon Chase. So Simone had kept her plans to herself.

For the first time, Hutch's facade cracked. His jaw firmed, and his eyes were bleak. "No one told me you had gotten married, Simone. Though, knowing you, I'm not surprised you kept your maiden name. Don't you want the baby's father to be here when we talk about these results? Can you contact him? We could reschedule for later this afternoon."

She stared at Hutch. "Have you read through my file?"

"Not yet. But I will, of course. All I've seen is the ultrasound report. I only came on board officially yesterday. To be honest, I'm still a little jet-lagged."

And no wonder. He'd spent the past half decade in Sudan with Doctors Without Borders. The man was almost too good to be true, strong, sensitive and—when he unleashed that boy-next-door charm—virtually irresistible.

Though they had no longer been a couple when

he left Royal, Texas, in the intervening months and years, she had worried about him. Malaria. Viral hemorrhagic fever. Political uprisings. He had thrust himself into a hotbed of danger and never looked back. Even without being there, Simone knew he had saved untold numbers of mothers and babies.

Hutch had completed not one but two stints in Sudan. When he hadn't returned after the first one, she knew for sure he was no longer interested in resurrecting their relationship—although that was possibly too mature a word for the affair. She and Hutch together had been like fireworks, burning hot and bright and beautiful, but over too soon.

While she mentally rehashed the painful past, Hutch waited patiently, his expression guarded. Having him eye her with the impassivity of a medical professional hurt. A lot.

Whipping up a batch of righteous indignation helped. It was none of Hutch's concern what she did with her life. "There is no father in the picture," she said bluntly. "Go ahead and tell me what you have to say."

For a split second, something flickered across his face. Shock? Probably. Relief? Unlikely.

"I'm sorry to hear that," he said, his tone so formal it could have frozen the air itself. "Are you divorced? Widowed?"

"I don't think you're supposed to ask me that, Dr. Hutchinson." She was furious suddenly—at herself for making such a mess of things, at Hutch for having the audacity to come home looking wonderful and completely unapproachable, if a bit tired, and at life in general.

He swallowed. "My apologies. You're right. That was out of line."

Despite her best intentions, she couldn't stay mad. Not today. And besides, what did it matter if she told him? Not the whole truth, of course. But he had her file at his disposal. Sooner or later, he would know. She might as well put a good spin on it.

"I wanted to have a baby," she said bluntly. *Maybe for all the wrong reasons, but still...* "I chose to use an anonymous sperm donor, because I had no significant other in the picture. This baby will be mine and mine alone. There are plenty of single mothers out there doing very well. I have a good job, financial resources and plenty of friends. I'll be able to handle motherhood, Hutch. You don't have to look at me like that."

Her decisions about parenthood and her grandfather's bequest were her own. She didn't want to be judged, and in truth, the facts could very easily be misinterpreted, leaving her in a bad light.

It was a real worry, particularly since the mysterious Maverick had somehow found out about her fertility treatments and threatened to expose her secrets. She pushed that situation to the back of her mind. Dealing with Hutch was enough drama for one day.

He stared at her with such intensity she felt oddly faint. Her heart beat loudly in her ears. Hutch's expression was a mixture of incredulity, pity and disapproval. Or at least that was how she interpreted it. At one time, she could guess what he was thinking. That was long ago, though.

Tossing the manila folder on the counter beside the computer, he shoved his hands in his pockets. "I

JANICE MAYNARD   13

have no doubts about your ability to care for a baby," he said.

She frowned. "Then why all the mystery? Why do you look like you're about to deliver words of doom? Is it something else? A tumor? Some weird cancer? Am I dying? That would suck."

His lips twitched. "Not at all, Simone. You're having triplets."

Hutch cursed when Simone went milk pale and keeled over. He caught her before she hit the floor, but just barely. Hell, he knew better. It wasn't the kind of news one delivered with a baseball bat. As usual, though, she rattled him. Even now.

Cradling her in his arms, he turned back to the exam table. His instinct was to hold her until she woke up. But that was all kinds of unethical. Instead, he laid her gently on her back and reached into the cabinet for a soft, mesh-weave blanket. Covering her all the way up to her neck, he tried not to notice the way she smelled. He could have identified her scent with his eyes closed. A mix of floral and spicy that was uniquely Simone.

She roused slowly, those incredibly long lashes fluttering as she came back to him. "What happened?"

When she tried to rise up onto her elbows, he put a hand on her shoulder to keep her down. "Give yourself a minute to recover. You've had a shock."

Even befuddled and wrapped in a generic blanket, she was striking. Her blue eyes were electric, somewhere between royal and aquamarine. Her hair made as much of an impact as her eyes. The smooth, silky fall was the black of a raven's wing…shot through with blue in the sunlight. He tried not to remember what it felt like to wrap his hands in all that thick, glorious hair. At one time, it had reached almost to her waist. The style was shorter now, but still a couple of inches below her shoulders.

Her gaze cleared gradually. "So I wasn't dreaming." The words were not really a question.

"No."

"I want to sit up."

He helped her, though it was difficult to touch her. She made him feel like a gawky adolescent. That was bloody uncomfortable for a man supposed to be in charge of Royal, Texas's world-class obstetrics department.

"I apologize for springing it on you, Simone. There's no easy way to drop that bomb. I have to tell you I'm surprised and concerned that you've chosen this option."

"I'm not getting any younger." The set of her jaw was mulish.

He remembered all too well what Simone was like when she made up her mind about something. "You're not even thirty. Couldn't you have waited and taken the traditional route?" he asked.

The wash of color that had returned to her face leached away again. Her eyes glittered with something that might have been pain or anger. "I tried that once or twice. I'm not a fan. Men complicate things."

The blunt retort was a direct shot at him. It found its mark. Clearly, Simone still blamed him for their breakup. He wanted to fight back, but it was pointless after all this time. His job wasn't to be her friend, or even her boyfriend. He was charged with overseeing her medical care.

"I suppose it's a moot point now," he said, feeling weary and discouraged. "Unless you've changed your mind. Do you want to terminate the pregnancy? If that's your decision, hospital staff would of course preserve your privacy."

Simone blinked. "Is that what *you* think I should do?"

He weighed his words carefully. "Having triplets is an enormous commitment, even for a two-parent family. You would be doing this alone."

She stared at him. Her restless fingers pleated the edges of the blanket. "I want these babies."

He cocked his head, trying to read her emotions. "You wanted *one* baby, Simone. I think you need to weigh the situation seriously. While it's still very early."

"There's nothing to consider. I made a choice. I have to live with the consequences."

"For the rest of your life."

Hot color streaked her cheekbones. "I know you think I'm flighty and impulsive and a lightweight. What you don't realize is that I've grown up a lot in the time you've been gone. I can do this."

"But why?" That's what confused him. It wasn't as if she was running out of time. Besides, she had never particularly struck him as the maternal type.

"My reasons are my business, Dr. Hutchinson. Am I free to go now?"

There were secrets in her eyes and in her heart. He knew it. The two of them might have been separated by time and distance for the past few years, but there had been a moment when he had known everything about her. Every thought. Every feeling. Every beat of her energetic, enthusiastic, passionate heart.

The Simone he knew jumped into life with both feet, usually via the deep end. She had her naysayers— Royal was a relatively small town with a long memory. Her youthful missteps had cost her. A reputation was a hard thing to shake. But he knew she had a good heart.

"Just hear me out. You should know, Simone, that a multiple pregnancy immediately puts you in the high-risk category. The hospital hired me for my expertise. I'll be overseeing your case indirectly. Dr. Fetter will alert me if any problems arise. Will that be a problem?"

Simone blinked. "Do you have any crackers?"

"Excuse me?" Had his hearing taken a hit in Sudan?

"I need saltines. I'm about to puke."

Oh, lord. "Hold on," he said. Opening the door to the hallway, he bellowed for a nurse. The poor woman must have sprinted, because she was back in two minutes with the crackers and a cup of ice chips.

He took them with muttered thanks, closed the door firmly and turned to Simone. She wasn't white anymore. More like a transparent shade of green. Grabbing a plastic basin from the cabinet, he put it in her lap and unwrapped the crackers. "Slowly," he said.

"Don't worry," she muttered. "I'm afraid to move."

"Poor baby." He'd seen pregnant women almost every day of his professional life, but none had ever touched him as deeply as this one. Without overthinking it, he put an arm behind her back to support her. "I'll hold the cracker," he said. "You nibble."

It was a measure of how miserable she was that she didn't fight him. No snappy comeback. No insistence she could feed herself. When she leaned into him, his heart actually skipped a beat. A huge neon sign flashed in his brain. *Warning! Warning!*

Even though he knew he couldn't get close to her again, his body betrayed him. She was so familiar, so delightfully feminine. Every caveman instinct he possessed told him to fight for her, to protect her. Women were tough, far tougher than men at times. Still, this Simone who had come to him today was at a low spot. He wanted to make it all right for her.

Yet he was the last person she needed. He'd suffered too much heartache, witnessed too much heartbreak to offer Simone anything resembling the love they had once shared.

She managed the first cracker and started on the second. In between bites, he offered the ice chips. Four crackers in each pack, eight in all. Eventually, she finished them.

"Thank you," she said. "I'm okay now."

It was patently untrue, but he took her words at face value. He handed her what was left of the cup of ice. "I have other patients to see," he said, wondering why the thought of leaving this room was so unappealing.

"I know," she said. "Go. I'm fine. I'm glad you didn't die in Africa."

He chuckled. "Is that all you have to say?"

"I don't want to add to your ego. I won't be surprised if the town makes you the patron saint of Royal. Saint Hutch. It has a ring to it, don't you think?"

"You're such a brat."

"Some things never change." Her teeth dug into her bottom lip.

Gradually, her color was returning to normal. The

doctor in him approved. "That's not true, Simone. Neither of us is who we were five years ago. I know I'm not."

She tucked a wayward strand of hair behind her ear. "Is that a polite warning? You're telling me not to get any ideas?" Her sidelong glance held a touch of wry mischief.

Even now, she had the power to shock him. While he'd been willing to dance around their painful past, Simone plunged right into the murky depths. Maybe she knew him better than he realized.

"I wasn't, but I probably should have."

"You're not my doctor."

"No. Not technically." He paused, weighing his words. "Perhaps this is presumptuous on my part, but you opened this can of worms. I knew we would see each other again, Simone. It was inevitable if I came home. But…"

"But you've moved on."

"Yes. I have." He didn't tell her the rest. He couldn't.

Simone nodded. "I understand, Hutch. I think it's obvious I have my hands full, too. Maybe we can be friends, though."

"Maybe." He let the lie roll off his lips. As much as he wanted to help her, he couldn't get close. Not again. "Are you okay now? The nausea's better?"

She handed him the basin. "False alarm. You're good at this. Maybe you should be a doctor."

His smile was genuine. Simone had always been able to make him laugh, even when he took himself too seriously. He reached in his pocket for a business card and scrawled his cell number on the back. "I need you to promise," he said, handing it to her.

"Promise what?" She handled the little rectangle as if it were a poisonous snake.

"I want you to promise that you'll call me immediately if you have any problems."

"What about Dr. Fetter?"

He shoved his hands in the pockets of his lab coat. "She's a busy doctor with a lot of patients."

"And you're not?"

They stared at each other in silence. "Hell, Simone. You're not making this easy."

"I don't understand you."

"We share a past. I want to make sure you and these babies are okay."

"Saint Hutch."

If that's what she wanted to think, he might as well let her. It was far better than the truth. "I care about you," he said quietly. "I mean it. Any hour. Night or day. This isn't a typical pregnancy. I want to hear you say it."

She lifted one shoulder in an elegant gesture he remembered well. "Fine. I promise. Are you happy now?"

He hadn't been happy for a very long time. "It will do. I'll be in touch, Simone. Take care of yourself."

Two

After the run-in with Hutch, the actual appointment with Dr. Fetter a week later was anticlimactic. The rules for a multiple pregnancy were pretty much the same as any pregnancy. Take vitamins. Sleep and rest the appropriate amount. Exercise every day. Report any spotting or bleeding.

That last bit was scary. Simone stared at the obstetrician as the woman entered notes on a laptop. "How often does that happen? Bleeding, I mean."

Dr. Fetter looked up over the top of her glasses. "Ten to twenty percent of all pregnancies end in miscarriage, Simone. With multiples, the risk is higher. Nevertheless, you shouldn't waste time worrying about it. Your ultrasound looks good, and we'll monitor you closely, much more so than a typical pregnancy warrants."

"I see." It was easy for the doctor to say *don't worry*. She wasn't the one carrying three brand-new lives.

Soon after that sobering conversation, Simone was back outside staring around in a daze at the nicely landscaped grounds of the hospital. *Triplets*. No matter how many times she repeated the word in her head, it didn't seem real. She'd had daydreams about pushing a stylish stroller with a tiny infant dressed in pink or blue. It was hard to fathom the reality of taking three babies out on the town.

She sat in her car for the longest time, telling herself everything was going to be okay. Her initial motives in getting pregnant had been less than pure. Was the universe punishing her for playing around with motherhood?

Despite evidence to the contrary, she was stunned to realize that she *wanted* these babies desperately. Not one of them, or two…but all three. Placing her palm flat on her abdomen, she tried to imagine what she was going to look like in a few months. With triplets, she could be huge.

Oddly, the thought wasn't as alarming as it should have been. For a woman who wore haute couture as a matter of course and worked hard to keep her body in shape, the fact that she was able to imagine herself as big as a blimp without hyperventilating showed personal growth.

At least that's what she told herself.

It was getting late. She was supposed to be at Naomi's condo in less than an hour. Naomi and Cecelia were making their signature jalapeño and shredded beef pizza. Normally, Simone gobbled down at least three pieces. How was she going to make it through the evening when the thought of food made her want to barf?

As she drove to the other side of town, she practiced what she was going to say. *By the way, I haven't had sex in months, but I'm pregnant with triplets.* Or how about *I ran into Hutch last week. I don't think I ever got over him.*

Already she was reconsidering her decision to keep Naomi and Cecelia in the dark. This was too hard to do alone. She needed someone to talk to…someone who would have her back. If she couldn't confide in her two best friends, she couldn't confide in anybody. Naomi and Cecelia had been her closest companions and confidantes since grade school. Still, she wasn't ready to spill *all* her secrets at once. She needed time to wrap her head around things. It was happening too fast.

As Simone entered her code on a keypad and rolled through the elegant gate, she noted the perfectly manicured grounds of the luxury condo complex. Naomi's privacy was protected here. Naomi Price was famous in Royal for any number of reasons. Her cable television show had been picked up nationally, so now she was dispensing style advice to women—and men— coast to coast.

Simone parked and walked up the path. When she rang the buzzer, Cecelia answered the door. "It's about time. Where have you been?"

Clearly, the question was rhetorical, because Cecelia disappeared into the kitchen, leaving Simone to put a hand over her mouth and gag at the smell of cooking meat. *Oh, lordy.* She fished a water bottle from the depths of her leather tote and took a cautious sip. If she wasn't ready to talk about the babies, she had to get her stomach under control. Otherwise, her secret wasn't going to be a secret for very long.

Gingerly, she rounded the corner and entered the kitchen. The room wasn't huge, but it was as stylish as the woman who hovered over the stove. Naomi had brown eyes and long copper-brown hair. She was charming and extremely pretty, but Simone knew her friend didn't understand how beautiful she was.

Cecelia, on the other hand, had bombshell looks and knew how to use them. Her platinum hair and long legs drew men in droves. Her company, To the Moon, produced high-end children's merchandise but had recently branched out to the adult furniture realm with the launch of Luna Fine Furnishings. Simone and her ad agency were currently producing a hard-hitting campaign designed to take Cecelia's company to the next level.

The other two women barely said hello at first. They were squabbling over the correct ratio of peppers to meat. At last, Naomi looked up. "Hey, hon. What's the matter with you? I've seen ghosts with more color."

That was the thing about good friends. They didn't sugarcoat things. "Just an upset stomach," Simone said. "I think I ate too much at lunch." Fortunately, meal prep took precedence and no one called her on the lie.

Normally, Simone would have offered to help, but right now she stayed as far away from the food as possible. When the large pizza was in the oven, the three women adjourned to the living room. Simone envied Naomi's innate sense of style. Her home was stunning but extremely comfortable.

Simone claimed a comfy chair and sat down gingerly. She'd always heard about morning sickness, but she had never imagined how wretched it could be. Tucking her legs beneath her, she tried to get comfortable.

Cecelia, on the other hand, hovered by the window. She was always a high-energy person. Today she practically vibrated with excitement.

Naomi took a sip of her Chardonnay and waved a hand. "What's up, Cecelia? You said we had to wait for Simone. She's here now. Don't keep us in suspense."

The tall blonde spun around, fumbled in her pocket and held out her hand. "Deacon proposed! And I'm pregnant."

After that dual announcement, much squealing ensued. Simone and Naomi hugged their friend and admired the ring. Deacon Chase was quite a catch. He'd lived in Europe for a decade, but had returned to Royal and purchased a beautiful country lodge on the outskirts of town. The gorgeous, self-made billionaire hotelier had confidence and charisma and a dimpled smile that broke hearts everywhere. As far as Simone was concerned, he was one of the few men alive who could handle Cecelia and not be intimidated by her looks and personality.

Clearly, now was not the time for Simone to share her own news. For one, she didn't want to steal Cecelia's thunder.

When the furor died down, they adjourned to the kitchen and dug into the freshly baked pizza. Simone's stomach cooperated enough for her to get down most of one piece, though she surreptitiously removed the jalapeños and wrapped them in a paper napkin. No point in tempting fate.

"So who's your doctor?" Simone asked. *Please don't let it be Hutch.*

"I'm seeing Janine Fetter. She's not real chatty or friendly, but I don't need that in a doctor. I want someone I can trust to take care of me and my baby. Dr. Fetter fits the bill."

Naomi shook her head. "I still can't believe it. This means we'll have to plan a baby shower."

Cecelia laughed. "Give it time. I'm still in my first trimester. Plenty of opportunity for that. Deacon and I are going to keep the news to ourselves for a while, but he knew I would have to tell you two."

"Well, I should think so," Naomi said. "We've never kept secrets from each other."

Simone grimaced inwardly. The trio's tight friendship had backfired in Royal at times. Some people referred to them as the mean girls. The label wasn't fair. They weren't mean. But when three women were extremely successful, attractive and high-profile, there were bound to be those who took potshots. The criticism had sharpened after Naomi, Cecelia and Simone had been admitted into the Texas Cattleman's Club.

Some diehards still thought women should be kept out. And *somebody* had started the rumor that Naomi, Cecelia and Simone could be behind the malicious blackmail messages various residents of Royal had been receiving via social media.

It wasn't true. Even Cecelia had received one of the blackmailer's threats. Simone, too, though she hadn't told anyone.

Later that evening as Simone drove home, she struggled with feelings of envy. Cecelia had a baby on the way and a wedding to plan. That meant Cecelia's situation was cause for celebration. Simone, on the other hand, was pregnant with triplets whose biological father was an unknown sperm donor.

Lots of people used sperm donors in situations of infertility. But those were loving couples who made a joint decision and were excited about the chance to bring a child into their home.

Simone had done it selfishly because of her grandfather's stupid, archaic will. Blinking back tears, she clutched the steering wheel and apologized to the three tiny sparks of life in her womb. "I swear I'll be a good mom," she whispered. "I would take it all back if I could, but now you're on the way, and I want to keep you. You'll find out soon enough that grown-ups make mistakes. Me, in particular."

It would have been nice to have someone say, "There, there, Simone. Don't be so hard on yourself. Everything will work out for the best. You'll see." Unfortunately, unless she confided in Naomi and Cecelia, no one in Royal was likely to fulfill the role of pep squad. She'd have to be her own cheerleader. First order of business would be enjoying a relaxing evening at home.

Her house was welcoming and warm, but in a whole different way than Naomi's. After the ad agency landed its third big client, Simone had moved out of her bland apartment and purchased a five-acre estate in Pine Valley. The place was ridiculously large for one person, but she loved it.

At least she would have plenty of room for a live-in nanny. Or maybe two. *Triplets!* How would she ever manage?

When she made the turn from the main road onto

her property, she noted with pride the way the flow-ering cherry trees lined the driveway. When the wind blew, tiny white petals fluttered down like snow. Spring in Royal, Texas, was her favorite time of year.

It was a surprise to see a black SUV parked on the curving flagstone apron at her front door. An even bigger shock was the man who stepped out to face her. Not bothering to put her small sports car in the garage, she slammed on the brakes and slid out from behind the wheel. "What are you doing here, Hutch?"

She hated the way her heart jumped when she saw him. Even without three babies on the way, she shouldn't get involved again. Given the current situ-ation, it would be emotional suicide to think she had any kind of chance with the good doctor.

In his muscular arms he held a medium-sized box. "I brought you some books from my medical library. I remembered how you like to research things on your own, so I thought you could take a look at these. Plenty of stuff here about multiple births, both from a medi-cal standpoint and from a practical parenting aspect."

"That's thoughtful of you," Simone said. "Do you offer this kind of service to all your patients?"

His lips quirked in a reluctant smile. "You're not my patient, remember?"

"True." She wasn't exactly sure what the proto-col was here. In any case, she couldn't leave the man standing outside. "Would you like to come in for some iced tea or a cola?"

"Decaf coffee?" he asked hopefully.

"That, too."

"I'm in."

She unlocked the front door and tossed her keys on

a table in the foyer. Hutch set the box on a chair and looked around with interest. "I like your house," he said. "It looks like you."

Simone made her way to the kitchen, painfully aware that he followed closely at her heels. "How so?" She opened the refrigerator to cool her hot face and to hide for a moment. Her heart raced at a crazy tempo.

"Modern. Stylish. Simple. Sophisticated."

Wow. Was that really how he saw her? While she put the coffee on to brew, Hutch perched on a stool at the bar. "Thank you," she muttered. Was he thinking about all the money she had spent while he was caring for sick babies in terrible poverty? Was his compliment actually a veiled criticism?

Maybe she was reading too much into a casual comment.

"Where will you live now that you're back?" she asked. "Somewhere near the hospital?"

"Actually," he said with a weary grin, "I'm going to be your neighbor. I'll be closing on the brick colonial down the road soon."

"Oh." She knew the house well. It was less than half a mile from her place. Was that a coincidence?

Hutch shrugged. "I'm too old for bachelor digs. I wanted to put down roots."

"No more Doctors Without Borders?"

"I don't think so. It's a young man's game. I gave it more than five years of my life. It's the best thing I've ever done, but it was time to come home."

"I'm sure your parents are delighted." Hutch's mother and father were both lawyers. They had raised their son to believe he could be or do anything he wanted. Hutch had excelled all the way through school, despite the occasional run-ins with bullies.

"They were over the moon when they heard."

"Must be nice. My mom and dad drop by only when they want to lecture me about something. Of course, you probably remember that." Her parents had been none too thrilled about their only daughter dating someone they hadn't handpicked for her. Neither Hutch nor Simone had let the veiled disapproval dissuade them.

Remembering the passionate affair and its inevitable end was something Simone managed to avoid. Mostly. But with Hutch in her kitchen, the memories came crashing back.

The two of them had met at a party at the Cattleman's Club. Simone had been barely twenty-two and ready to fall in love. The town had thought she was promiscuous—still did—but that was a facade she hid behind. If people wanted to look down their noses at her, she wasn't going to stop them.

Being introduced to Troy Hutchinson by a mutual acquaintance had been kismet. The moment she laid eyes on him, she knew he was the one. Though he was ridiculously handsome, it was his quiet, steady intelligence that drew her in. Hutch was no callow boy looking for an easy lay.

He had talked to her, listened to her opinions. Danced with her. Laughed at her jokes. And in a secluded corner outside the club, he had kissed her. Even now she could remember everything about that magical moment. The way he smelled of lime and starched cotton. The sensation of feeling small and protected, though she was more than capable of taking care of herself. He was taller than she was and extremely fit, which made sense, of course, for someone who had devoted himself to the pursuit of medicine.

"Simone? Hello in there…"

Suddenly he was standing in front of her, his smile quizzical. "You've been stirring that cup of coffee for a long time."

Heat flooded her cheeks. Did he know what she was thinking? Could he read her mind?

"Here," she said. "I fixed it the way you like it. Strong enough to peel paint and enough sugar to give you cavities."

He took the cup and sipped slowly, his eyes closing in bliss. "Now *this* is good coffee. Might even compete with the real stuff in Africa."

"I'm sure not everything was great. As I recall, you were a meat-and-potatoes guy, too. Not much prime beef where you were, I'd say."

"You're right, of course. I lost twenty pounds after I arrived in Sudan and never quite gained it back."

"Let's take our drinks into the den." She grabbed a package of cookies out of the cabinet and led the way. Hutch chose a wing-backed chair near the dormant fireplace. Simone claimed one end of the sofa.

He sat back with a sigh, balancing his cup on his flat abdomen. "You've done well for yourself, Simone. I'm proud of you. Everyone in town sings your praises—well, your ad agency's praises," he clarified.

"That might be a stretch, but thanks. Hard work and a dollop of luck."

"I always knew you'd make your mark in Royal."

She frowned. Her ambition had been partly the cause of their breakup, but not from her perspective. She hadn't wanted to stand in the way of Hutch's dreams. When he'd offered to wait on Africa until her agency was established, she had insisted he should go. Hutch read that as a rejection. He thought she cared more about her business and money than about him. Stupid man.

Still, that was a long time ago.

For several long minutes they drank their coffee in silence. She was tired and queasy and sad. Seeing Hutch again was a painful reminder of how many times in her life she had made mistakes.

Would she ever learn?

At last, the silence became unbearable. She set her cup on a side table. "I think you should go now," she said. "I don't feel very well. I'd like to rest. And if I'm being honest, I'd rather not have people see your car in front of my house."

Three

Hutch grimaced. Her words stung, even though they gave him an easy out.

He had told himself he was indifferent to Simone now, but in his gut he knew the truth. The first moment he laid eyes on her in that exam room a week ago, he'd felt the same dizzying punch of desire he'd always experienced when he was with her.

Panic swept through him like a sickening deluge. He couldn't do that again. Not after what had happened in Sudan. It was better that Simone knew the score.

She lost patience with his lack of verbal response. "If you have something to say, say it. I've had a long, stressful day, and I want to take a bath and get into bed."

I'd like to join you... His subconscious was honest and uncomfortable.

The dark shadows beneath her beautiful eyes reminded him she was in a fragile state, both mentally and physically.

The fact that he wanted so badly to hold her told him he had to protect himself.

He stood and paced, his hands jammed in his pockets. "I understand why you want me to move my car. Now that I'm back in town and we're both still single, the gossip mill will undoubtedly have us hooking up any day now. People may even say your triplets are mine."

Simone swallowed visibly. "Gossip isn't reality."

"Maybe not. But I have to be up front with you. I'm not willing to get involved in a relationship."

She was pale and silent, her sapphire-eyed stare judging him. "I don't recall asking you to. But to clarify, is your distaste for romance because of our past?"

"Not entirely. I fell in love with a fellow doctor while I was in Sudan. Her name was Bethany."

For a split second, he could swear he saw anguish in Simone's eyes. But if it was there, she recovered quickly.

"You said was? Past tense?"

He nodded jerkily. "She died two years ago. Cut her foot on a rock. Doctors make the worst patients, you know. She didn't tell any of us how serious it was. Ended up with sepsis. I couldn't save her." Even now the memory sickened him.

Simone leaned forward. "I am so sorry, Hutch."

Her sympathy should have soothed him. Instead, it made him feel guilty. "I'll always be fond of you, Simone…and I'll care about you. But I need you to know that's all it will be."

She blinked. "I see."

"I suppose you think I'm assuming a hell of a lot to think you would even be interested after all this time."

"Not at all. You're a gorgeous man. With a kind heart. I'm sure I won't be the only woman in Royal who appreciates your sterling qualities."

"Aw, hell. You're making fun of me, aren't you?"

"Maybe a little." She smiled gently. "Six months ago your virtue might have been in danger. But now I have three babies to consider. Their welfare has to come before anything else in my life."

"Even romance?"

"Especially romance."

"Then I guess we've cleared the air."

"I guess we have."

"I should go," he said. But he didn't move.

Simone stood up, swaying a bit before she steadied herself with a hand on the back of the chair. "Yes, you should."

Squaring his shoulders, he nodded. The urge to kiss her was overpowering.

She kept a hand on the chair, either because she felt faint or because she intended to use it as a shield. Either way, it didn't matter. He wanted to taste her more than he wanted his next breath.

He put his hands on her shoulders, noting the tension there. She wasn't wearing shoes, so the difference in their heights was magnified. Winnowing his fingers through her hair, he sighed. "I should have come home a year ago. Then maybe I could have talked you out of this single-mom idea."

"Not your business, Doc."

It was as easy as falling into a dream. He had loved

Bethany, deeply and truly. And grieved her passing. But this thing with Simone was something else. Did he dare explore the possibilities?

Slowly, he moved his lips over hers, waiting for the protest that never came. She tasted of coffee and wonderful familiarity. But not comfort. Never comfort. There was too much heat. Too much yearning. When she went up on her tiptoes and wrapped her arms around his neck, he groaned. Five years. Almost six. Gone in a flash.

He ran his hands over her back and landed on her bottom. She was thinner, but every bit as soft and appealing as she had ever been. Before he left for Sudan, when they were alone together, Simone had been unguarded…innocent. A far cry from the woman who tilted her chin and dared the world to disrespect her.

Every beat of his heart was magnified. He kissed the sensitive spot behind her ear…nipped her earlobe with his teeth. Simone did nothing to stop him. In fact, she didn't even try to hide the fact that she wanted him. Temptation sank its teeth into his gut and didn't let go. He was hard as a pike. The sofa was close by. Damn. How could he still want her so badly? No. This had to stop. Now.

Dragging in great gulps of air, he broke free of the embrace, stumbled backward and wiped a hand over his mouth. "Does it make you happy to know I still want you?" he snarled. He felt like a fool.

Simone's expression was gaunt and defeated. "Not happy at all, Hutch. But message received. You have nothing to fear from me. I'd appreciate it if you would let yourself out."

* * *

She waited until she heard the front door slam before bursting into tears. Sliding down the wall and curling up in a knot of misery on the hallway floor, she cried ugly, wretched sobs that left her throat raw and her chest hollow.

She knew her hormones were all over the map, but it was more than that. Hutch might as well still be in Africa. The gulf between them was so deep and so wide, it was doubtful they could ever even manage to be friends. Yet the same incendiary attraction that had drawn them to each other in the beginning still existed.

The sensation of being wrapped in his strong arms…of feeling his steady heartbeat beneath her cheek…of knowing he wanted her as much as she wanted him brought back such crazy joy. Never in her life had she felt as happy or free as she had when she and Hutch were a couple.

What he said was true. If he had come home six months ago, she would never have embarked on this path of insanity. She'd been angry at her dead grandfather and determined to prove she was worthy of carrying on the family name. It had never been about the money, but more about legitimacy, a sense of belonging.

Now it was too late for second thoughts. The babies were a reality.

Stumbling to her bathroom, she washed her face and sprawled on the bed. She was hungry again, but it was a weird hunger. Beneath the pangs of an empty stomach rolled a sensation of nausea in the offing.

Finally, at midnight, she dragged herself out of bed and went to the kitchen in search of a snack. Milk seemed like a bad idea. Ditto for cheese or yogurt. Craving something salty, she found half a bag of stale, plain potato chips. She gobbled two handfuls and washed them down with ginger ale.

Her hunger appeased, she went back to bed only to jump up twenty minutes later and rush for the bathroom. She threw up violently, so hard that her ribs ached. Even rinsing out her mouth made her stomach heave.

Groaning, she found a damp cloth and pressed it to her forehead. The notion that she might have to endure weeks of this misery pointed out once again how foolish she had been. *I'm sorry*, she said silently to the three lives she carried.

No matter what sacrifices it demanded, she would make sure this was a healthy pregnancy.

The following morning was no better. Dry cereal and water came right back up as soon as they went down. Her hands began to cramp, signaling possible dehydration. Doggedly, she sipped from a water bottle and forced herself to put on the same dress pants from the day before but with a different top. She couldn't simply stay home because she felt bad. She had a business to run…a business that would soon support three tiny infants.

Driving was doable, but only because she never pushed the speedometer over thirty miles an hour. When she reached her office, the receptionist, Candace, gave her a wide-eyed stare. Simone didn't engage. She made a beeline for her private suite, closed the door and put her head on the desk. The sharp corner of a business card poked her stomach through her pocket.

She pulled the rectangle out and laid it on the desk. Hutch. Dr. Hutch. Saint Hutch. It would be a cold day in hell before she called him for *anything*.

With nothing more than dogged determination and the inherent stubbornness that got her into trouble more often than not, she made it through an entire workday. The campaign for Luna Fine Furnishings, a subsidiary of Cecelia's company, To the Moon, was coming along nicely. Phase one had already been rolled out. In two weeks, an intensive social media blitz would back up the initial print ads and billboards.

The noon lunch hour came and went. Simone didn't even attempt to eat. At five o'clock, she closed her laptop, packed up her things and took a deep breath before heading out to her car. Once there, she had to spend another chunk of time convincing herself she could make the drive home. She was shaky, light-headed and so very sick.

She must have dozed when she got home, because suddenly it was seven o'clock. Naomi would bring her food if she called, but then Simone would have to explain what was going on. Even if it was time to share her secret with her friends, she'd rather do it with both women present.

Carryout pizza sounded revolting. Canvassing the pantry in her kitchen was an exercise in futility. She knew *how* to cook but seldom spared the time. Most days she had lunch with clients and grabbed a salad for dinner.

In the end, the only available choice was peanut butter. That was protein—right? Even her crackers were stale. But smeared with peanut butter, they were edible. At first, Simone thought she had landed on a miracle. The peanut butter was comfort food, its smell and taste appealing.

Sadly, no matter the enjoyment going down, everything she consumed came back up in a matter of minutes.

The night passed slowly. She alternated between lying on top of the covers covered in a cold sweat and hunching over the toilet. No matter how slowly she sipped water, it wouldn't stay down. Nor would anything else.

Once she almost fell, so dizzy the room spun around her. Finally, at 4:00 a.m., she collapsed into an exhausted slumber.

When her alarm went off, she muttered an incredulous protest. How did working mothers do this?

Dragging herself into the shower, she held on to the towel bar as she washed her hair. Blow-drying it took everything she had. At last she was dressed and ready to go. By now the thought of trying to eat was beyond her. Maybe she'd be able to attempt some lunch.

The ride to work was a blur. This time she barely noticed the receptionist's look of consternation. Simone's mouth was dry and fuzzy. How could she risk taking a drink when she might have to rush for the bathroom? No one in Royal knew she was pregnant. Well, aside from Hutch and Dr. Fetter. It was far too early to let that cat out of the bag.

As she sat in a stupor at her desk, the buzzer on her phone sounded. "Line two, Ms. Parker. It's your accountant."

Later, Simone couldn't remember the exact details of that conversation. For all she knew, she might have agreed to transfer her personal and business funds to illegal offshore accounts.

Thankfully, her two full-time employees—including her exceptional right hand, Tess—were out of town at a conference. The receptionist was fairly new and wouldn't have the temerity to invade her office uninvited.

So the hours passed.

At one, Simone knew she had to eat something. Her headache had reached monumental proportions. Maybe she would send Candace out to get chicken noodle soup. Not only would that guarantee Simone a few minutes of privacy to test her stomach with a sip of water, but the soup might actually be good for her.

She stood up on trembling legs. Rarely did she ask an employee to carry out a personal errand, but she was literally incapable of walking down the block. Carefully, she opened her door. "Candace, can you come in here?"

Candace looked up and blanched. Apparently Simone looked even worse than she felt. Her receptionist rushed into the office. "Can I help you, Ms. Parker?" she asked.

Simone nodded, wincing when the motion sent shock waves through her skull. "Would you mind grabbing me some chicken soup from the diner?"

"I'd be happy to," Candace said.

"Let me get my billfold."

"No worries. We can settle up later. Do you want something to drink? Lemonade? Iced tea?"

Oh, wow. Tea sounded wonderful. "Tea would be great." Her mouth was so dry. "Hurry, Candace. I don't think I can—" She stopped dead, nausea rising in her throat. "Oh, damn. I'm going to—"

It might have been hours or days later when she woke up completely. She had vague memories of an ambulance and several people in white coats. Now she was in her own bed.

When she shifted on the mattress, Hutch's voice sounded nearby. "Take it easy, Simone. You're going to be okay."

"My head hurts," she groaned, trying to recreate her spotty memory.

"No wonder." Hutch crouched beside her bed, his smile quizzical. "You whacked it pretty hard on the edge of your desk when you fainted. The ER doc put in three stitches, but there's no concussion."

Panicked, she tried to sit up. "The babies?"

"Steady, woman. They're fine."

"What happened to me?"

"Hyperemesis gravidarum."

"Oh, God. Is that as bad as it sounds?"

"Yes and no. You were badly dehydrated, Simone, and disoriented. One of the unlucky women who suffer from severe nausea and vomiting when pregnant. Women with multiples are more prone to it."

"Well, that's just peachy," she muttered.

"Dr. Fetter wanted to admit you, but you pitched a fit and demanded to go home. She only agreed because I promised to stay with you."

For the first time, Simone realized she was hooked up to an IV. "You did this?"

He looked at her strangely. "Yes. But if you've changed your mind, I'll take you back to the hospital."

Now that her head was clearer, she did remember most of what he was saying. It didn't paint her in a good light.

"How did you hear I had passed out? Why were you there with the EMTs? Candace doesn't even know you."

"She was trying to call 911 and saw my card on your desk."

"I knew I should have thrown that away."

Hutch had the audacity to laugh. When he did, she caught a glimpse of the carefree young doctor she had fallen in love with so many years ago. Heaven help her. With the shadows gone from his eyes—chased away by genuine humor—he was irresistible.

He fiddled with a setting on the monitor. "It will take at least twenty-four hours to get your electrolyte levels balanced again. After that, we'll have to see if you are able eat or drink at all. Otherwise, you'll have to get nutrition intravenously."

"How long will this last?"

"Well…" It was clear he didn't want to upset her.

"Go ahead, Hutch. I can handle it."

"Days. Weeks." He grimaced. "For some it's all the way till the end. But you're in the earliest moments of this pregnancy. Your body is adapting to the flood of hormones. With any luck, things will settle down soon."

"Thanks for the pep talk," she said drily. She watched as he moved around the bedroom. "You can't stay here. You have a job."

"I was going to talk to you about that. I have a friend, a nurse, who does in-home care. She's expensive, but it's cheaper than being hospitalized and a lot more comfortable."

"She would stay overnight?"

Hutch rubbed two fingers in the center of his forehead. "No. I would be here when I get off work in the evenings."

Simone closed her eyes and told herself not to get upset. That wouldn't be good for the babies. "You know that's impossible," she whispered.

He sat down on the edge of the bed and took her hand, the one with the needle taped into it. "My job is to protect high-risk infants. What happened to you is serious, but there's no reason to take up a hospital bed."

"What about staying away from each other?"

"You're all hooked up. How bad could we be?"

The droll comment startled a laugh from her when she could have sworn she didn't have it in her. "I have friends," she said. "And parents."

"Don't be coy, Simone. I happen to know that Cecelia is newly engaged and pregnant and Naomi flits all over the country. Your parents wouldn't begin to know how to be nurturing. I've met them, remember? I'm your best shot if you want to stay out of the hospital."

Well, damn. The idea of checking into a hospital for something like this gave her the hives. "You could teach me about the IV," she said, giving him a hopeful glance.

"Nice try, kiddo. Even Kate Middleton had to stay in the hospital a few nights when she struggled with this condition. Despite the fact that she had castles and servants at her disposal. Count yourself lucky that Dr. Fetter trusts me."

"She should. You're her boss."

"You know what I mean."

"I'm sorry Candace dragged you into this."

He leaned over and brushed a strand of hair from her cheek. "I'm not. You gave everyone a real scare. I'd just as soon be the one keeping an eye on you."

Four

Hutch kept his easy smile with effort. Never had he imagined seeing Simone in the state she'd been in when she collapsed. Severe dehydration could even affect the heart. When he'd first seen her, he had actually feared for her pregnancy.

Not only that, he had flashed back to losing Beth. Even though he didn't want a romantic relationship with Simone again, there was no way in hell he was going to let anything happen to her on his watch.

The stubborn woman had to have been in misery. Yet she'd been determined to power through on her own. She looked a little better now, but not much. He estimated that she had already lost six or seven pounds. Her cheekbones stood out sharply, as did her collarbone.

He touched the spot beneath her ear. "They put

motion-sickness patches on you in the hospital. I'll change those out as necessary."

"Is it safe?" Her fingers moved restlessly, pleating the sheet.

He frowned. "A hell of a lot safer than collapsing from dehydration. You were in a bad way, Simone."

"I thought I could handle it."

"You hate depending on other people for help, don't you?"

"I don't like to take help from *you*." Tears welled in her beautiful eyes, making them sparkle.

He sat down again, telling himself he had to be the professional in this situation. "I owe you this much, don't you think?"

"For what?" She couldn't quite meet his eyes.

"For taking your advice and going to Africa." He couldn't help the fact that the words sounded accusatory. When it had become clear that he and Simone were crazy about each other, he had offered to linger in Royal for a few years until she got her ad agency off the ground. He'd assumed she would jump at the offer. Instead, she had broken up with him. She'd insisted she didn't want to stand in the way of his doing something so important.

Bitter and disillusioned, he had realized that Simone didn't love him the way he loved her. While he couldn't bear the thought of leaving her behind, she had cut him loose and bid him a cheerful farewell.

"I did the right thing," she said stubbornly. "You had a mission to fulfill."

"And what did *you* have, Simone?" Suddenly, he felt like a beast for harassing her. She looked fragile enough to shatter. "Forget I said that," he muttered. "I'm sorry. It's not important."

Without warning, a noise from the front of the house had his head jerking up. Surely no one would barge in uninvited. But he had forgotten about Naomi. The style guru/TV star was as much a force of nature as Simone, though in a different package.

Naomi burst into the bedroom, wild-eyed. She barely glanced at Hutch. "Good lord, Simone. What the heck is going on? I just saw you a few days ago. What happened?"

Hutch moved toward the door. "I'll leave you two ladies alone."

Simone held up the hand that wasn't tethered to an IV. "No. Don't go, Hutch. You might as well both hear this at once."

Naomi turned to frown at him. "I didn't know you were back in town. Made yourself at home, didn't you? I fail to see why you're in this house. You hurt her enough the first time around. I'm here now. You can leave."

Simone tried to sit up. "Hush, Naomi. You don't know what you're talking about. Ignore her, Hutch. You know how dramatic she can be."

Naomi's teeth-clenched smile promised retribution. She sat down on the side of the bed, careful not to jostle Simone. "Fine. What don't I know?"

Hutch positioned himself at Simone's elbow. "You don't have to do this now, Simone. You're weak and sick." He worried about her state of mind.

She shot him a look that held a soupçon of her usual fire. "I'm not an invalid." Reaching for Naomi's hand, she twined their fingers. "Don't be mad. I didn't want to steal Cecelia's thunder the other night. I'm pregnant, too. And apparently not handling it nearly as well as our newly engaged friend."

The self-derision on her face hurt Hutch. "It's not a contest," he said.

Naomi gaped. "You're pregnant?" She glared at Hutch.

He held up his hands. "Don't look at me."

"Then who?" Naomi seemed genuinely befuddled.

Maybe Simone had been telling the truth about not having a man in her life. That shouldn't have pleased him so much. Simone tried to sit up again, and again, he shook his head. "Too soon. Stay put."

"Fine. Anyone ever tell you you worry too much?" She transferred her attention to her shell-shocked friend. "I wanted to have a baby, Naomi. And I didn't want to wait. So I used a sperm donor."

"A sperm donor…" Naomi repeated the words slowly.

"Don't look so stunned," Simone pleaded. "It's a perfectly acceptable thing to do."

"But it's not something the Simone *I* know would do."

Hutch saw Simone's bottom lip tremble. "That's enough, Naomi," he said. "This has been a rough day for her."

"Sorry," she groaned. "What's the matter with her?"

"She's suffering from extreme morning sickness."

"I'm right here," Simone snapped. "And I don't know why they call it morning sickness. It lasts the whole damn day."

He and Naomi looked at each other, trying not to laugh. Hutch lifted a shoulder, edging toward the door.

"I really do have some phone calls to make." He looked at Naomi. "Shout if you need me."

In the kitchen, he prowled restlessly. Neither of the phone calls was urgent, but he had needed some space to clear his head. He already regretted his impulsive decision to take on Simone's crisis. The odd thing was, *she* was the one who usually jumped without looking. There was a time when he had admired her joie de vivre and her impulsive spirit.

He'd been the older one, the stick-in-the-mud. He'd often wondered if that was why she broke up with him. Perhaps his overly conscientious approach to life had struck her as boring and pedantic.

It didn't matter now. If they hadn't had anything in common five years ago, that was even more true now. Hopefully, her nausea would soon settle down and he could go back to pretending she was just another pregnant woman.

Simone looked at Naomi. "Help me sit up, please."

Naomi frowned. "Hutch said that wasn't a good idea."

"Are you kidding me? Since when are you in the Troy Hutchinson fan club?"

"I didn't say I was a fan, but the man's a brilliant doctor, and you, my girl, look like something out of a zombie movie."

"Gee, thanks."

Despite her protests, Naomi stood up and grabbed extra pillows to put behind Simone. "Satisfied?"

Simone closed her eyes. "I'll be satisfied when I can eat a milk shake and a cheeseburger without puking."

"Can I get you anything?" Naomi hovered.

"No. Thank you." Unexpected tears stung her eyes. "I feel so stupid."

Naomi chuckled. "Well, you should. If anybody was going to knock you up, it should have been that Greek god doctor of yours."

"He's not my doctor," Simone said automatically. "And besides, we're not anything to each other."

"Which explains why I found him in bed with you."

"Don't be dramatic. He wasn't *in* my bed. He was *sitting* on my bed. There's a big difference."

"Not from where I'm standing."

"For God's sake, let it go, Naomi. Hutch and I were over a long time ago. And besides, even if I had the slightest interest in rekindling that flame—which I don't—what man wants to be father to some other guy's triplets?"

Naomi gaped. The look of total consternation on her face might have been funny if Simone hadn't felt so wretched. "Triplets?" she said, her eyes round.

"Um, yeah. I guess I forgot to mention that part. I'm having three babies. At least I hope so."

"What does that mean?"

"It's still early. Too early to know if all the fetuses are viable."

Naomi sprang to her feet and paced. "How can you be so damned calm? This is huge. What were you thinking, Simone? You own and manage a thriving ad agency. You have no husband. Why on earth would you do something so crazy?"

Sadly, Simone couldn't tell the whole truth. Not to Naomi or Cecelia, and certainly not to Hutch. "I wanted a baby," she said stubbornly. "By the time I got in the midst of everything, I began to have my doubts, but I didn't back out. I should have, I suppose."

"Ya think?" Naomi seemed more indignant than flat-out angry. Simone understood, really, she did. If the situations had been reversed, surely she would have expressed doubts about Naomi's decision.

"I screwed up, Naomi. I know that now. But I didn't know how sick I could get. And besides…"

"Besides, what?"

"I want them," Simone whispered. "The babies. All of them. Hutch said it wasn't too late from a medical standpoint to rethink my position, but I could never do that. I started this, and I'll finish it."

Naomi pursed her lips. "I hope it doesn't finish *you*."

Hutch returned in time to hear that last comment. He frowned when he saw Simone upright, but he didn't say anything.

Simone looked at him. "May I have a drink of water, please?"

"It's up to you. It would be good if you can manage it."

With both of them watching, Simone didn't want to make a scene, but she knew she couldn't avoid drinking indefinitely. There was a pitcher and disposable cups on the bedside table. Hutch poured one glass half-full and offered it to her. She took it from him, wincing. "Bottoms up."

With her two observers looking on eagle-eyed, she sipped tentatively. At first, the water tasted amazing. Her lips were partially chapped. The cool liquid felt wonderful in her parched throat. But moments later, her stomach cramped sharply. "Hutch!" She panicked.

He was there immediately, holding a small basin as the water came back up and she retched helplessly. Hutch held her hair. Naomi produced a damp cloth for her forehead. *Oh, God.* If she had ever felt so humiliated and miserable, she couldn't remember it.

Hutch didn't wait for permission. He removed the pillows and helped her lie flat again. "Okay now?" he asked.

She nodded, unable to look at either of them. "I'm sorry to drag you both into this."

Naomi forced a laugh that sounded almost natural. "C'mon, girl. We've been through a lot of rough patches together over the years. Cecelia and I will help. And you're not poor. That's a plus."

Even Hutch thought that was funny, though he quickly turned his chuckle into a cough. It was probably not acceptable bedside manner to make jokes at the patient's expense.

"Hilarious." Suddenly, it struck her. "Well, crud. I'll never fit into a slinky bridesmaid dress."

Even Naomi didn't have the chutzpah to pretend that wasn't true. But she tried to put a spin on it. "Maybe they'll elope. You never know."

Hutch spoke up, for the first time sounding more like a doctor than an interested party. "I'm glad you came by, Naomi. I'll keep you posted if anything changes. Simone needs to rest now."

Simone wanted to argue that he was being high-handed, but it was the truth. "I should tell Cecelia the news in person," she said.

"No worries." Naomi gathered up her car keys and cell phone. "I'll take care of it. She'll understand."

That wasn't the problem. *No one* was going to understand unless Simone's original motive was revealed. Then she was in big trouble. "Thank you, Naomi."

"Anything for a friend." With a wave and a smile, she was gone.

In the silence that followed Naomi's departure, Simone tried to pretend Hutch had left, as well. Unfortunately, he was impossible to ignore.

Simone loved her bedroom, as a rule. She had always found it soothing with its color scheme of pale lemon yellow and navy. It wasn't too girly.

Today, though, with Hutch in residence, the charming space felt claustrophobic. "How long do I have to have the IV?"

"Until you can take nourishment of some kind. I'll show you how to unhook and stop the monitor from beeping when you need to go to the bathroom. You'll have to promise me, though, that you'll hold on to something and sit down the moment you feel dizzy. Otherwise, I'm going in there with you."

"Over my dead body." Her whole body flushed.

He didn't bother arguing that one.

"You look tired," she said impulsively.

Hutch half turned, his striking face in profile. "It's been a tough day," he said.

"Surely not as tough as Sudan."

"Tough in a different way. You need to sleep now, Simone."

"It's only seven o'clock. Have you eaten?"

"I'll get something later."

"Go now," she urged. "I swear I won't move until you get back."

He shook his head, his expression wry. "I'm not

sure I trust you. For the next seventy-two hours, you're my responsibility."

"What am I supposed to do if I can't eat or drink or get out of bed?"

"How about a movie?"

"Will you watch it with me?"

His dark gaze made her shiver, despite her weakened state. He closed his eyes, took a deep breath and dropped his chin to his chest. After a moment, he lifted his shoulders and let them fall, then looked at her with a carefully blank expression. "If that's what you want. I'll go make myself a sandwich. Here's the remote. You pick something out and I'll be back shortly."

She channel surfed halfheartedly, feeling almost normal for the moment. The pregnancy didn't seem entirely real. Was that odd? Shouldn't she feel a rush of maternal devotion? She did have a connection already. She knew life was growing in her womb even now. But those little blips on the screen didn't have faces and personalities. What if they grew up to be like her?

Eventually, she found a Tom Hanks romantic comedy from the '80s in the on-demand section. That would do the trick. She and Hutch could make fun of the sappy dialogue. At least that's what she told herself. Never in a million years would she let him know how much she loved that story.

When he came back from the kitchen, he had his hands full. He stopped in the doorway as if expecting to find her flouting his orders. She smiled innocently. "I've been good as gold."

"That'll be the day."

Her bed was a king, so when Hutch parked himself on the opposite side, there was an entire stretch of mattress protecting her virtue. Not that it mattered. Who was she kidding? She'd seen herself in the mirror.

Hutch got comfortable and began to wolf down his meal. Suddenly he looked at her in dismay. "Will the smell bother you? I can eat in the kitchen."

"No. I'm fine. If you were eating Thai food, it might be different. That ham sandwich is nausea neutral."

She started the movie, trying not to notice the way Hutch seemed entirely comfortable in her bed. When they had been a couple, she had lived in an upscale apartment downtown, as had Hutch. They'd split their time between locations, some nights in his bed, some nights in hers.

The sex had been incredible, but even more than that was the feeling of rightness… She didn't know how else to explain it. In the beginning, they had talked for hours. She learned that Hutch decided to go into medicine after an older cousin had a difficult pregnancy when he was in high school. The mother and baby both died. Thus, maternal-fetal medicine became his focus when it was time to specialize.

Simone had been out of college barely a year when she met Hutch. She'd worked for a high-end clothing store as a buyer. Marketing was her passion, though, and she'd spent many hours telling Hutch about her intent to open an advertising agency of her own.

Aside from that, they had, of course, talked about their families. Simone was an only child. Hutch had a younger brother who was studying abroad and hoped to go into the diplomatic corps.

Hutch's parents were warm and nurturing, whereas Simone's were strict and cold. Though it was a sad cliché, her father had wanted a boy. But complications during her mother's pregnancy meant no more children after Simone. No matter how hard Simone tried, she never seemed to measure up to a list of invisible standards.

Perhaps that was why she reveled in Hutch's attention. Not that she saw him as a father figure. Far from it. The age difference was too narrow for that. But when she spoke, he took her seriously. It was heady stuff.

In her peripheral vision, she could see that Hutch's attention was focused on the television. Was he really engrossed in the movie? She doubted it. More likely, he was thinking about important doctor stuff.

Unlike Simone's endeavors, Hutch's work actually involved life-and-death situations. She teased him about being a saint, but she had never met another man who impressed her so deeply with his work ethic and his compassion.

If he had stayed, they might have ended up married, and Hutch's involvement with DWB might never have materialized. In Simone's twenty-eight years, many people in her life had characterized her as self-centered. Sadly, that had probably been true at one time. But at least she had the comfort of knowing that in this instance she had done the right thing.

She had loved Hutch madly, deeply, desperately... but she had let him go.

When the memories stung too sharply, she hit the mute button on the remote and silenced the TV. "I've seen this one a dozen times," she said. "What I'd really like is for you to tell me about Bethany. And about Sudan."

Five

Hutch froze. He'd been a million miles away. Simone's question caused him to flinch inwardly. Unfortunately, he couldn't think of an excuse to deflect it quickly enough.

"Why?" he asked bluntly.

Simone turned on her side and tucked her hands beneath her cheek. She was drowsy. He could hear it in her voice and see it in her eyes. "You were gone for a long time. Two tours of service. Why didn't you come home after the first one?"

It was a logical question. That had been the assumption all along. Still, when the time came, the thought of returning to Royal and confronting Simone had seemed far more dangerous than anything he would face abroad. So he had stayed.

A month later, he'd met Bethany.

Sensing that Simone wouldn't be dissuaded, he steeled himself for the pain and remorse that choked him when he allowed himself to remember. "I was introduced to Bethany just as I signed up for a second rotation. All the medical staff I had worked with were headed home. Bethany was one of the newbies."

"A nurse?"

"No. A doctor. A pediatrician. Bethany was the daughter of medical missionaries in Central America. She had never lived in the United States full-time until she went to college and med school. She adored children. Wanted five or six of her own one day. In the meantime, her goal was to save as many as she could in Sudan, specifically West Darfur, the state where we were stationed."

"Admirable."

"You would have liked her, I think. She was only five foot one, but somehow you never noticed that about her, because her personality was so compelling. She was passionate about her work and truly believed she was fulfilling her destiny."

"You said you fell in love," Simone prompted him with an expression that was difficult to read.

He stretched his arms over his head, feeling the fatigue of a long day. The last thing he wanted to do was rehash his past with Simone. Especially when it came to talking about another woman. But Simone was relentless when she wanted something.

"I fell in love," he said flatly. "It was slow. At first we were only friends. But I was lonely. I had been in Sudan for a long time."

"And Bethany?"

"I don't know what she saw in me," he said. "It certainly wasn't a romantic situation. Sometimes I think we were just two people doing the best we could."

Simone shifted restlessly. "You don't have to tell me any more, Hutch. She sounds like a lovely person. I'm sorry you lost her. Another day I'd like to hear about your work, but not tonight. I'm tired. I think I can sleep now."

He nodded. "I'll bunk on the sofa. I've programmed my cell number in your phone. Just buzz me when you need to get up."

"I have four perfectly lovely guest rooms, Hutch. You're way too big for the sofa."

He grimaced. "After the past five-plus years, I can sleep pretty much anywhere, trust me."

"But why would you?" Simone frowned.

It seemed cruel to be blunt when she was so sick, but it was better for him to draw the line in the sand. Better, and necessary. "You said it yourself, Simone— you know the way gossip spreads in Royal. It's important to me not to create the impression that I've moved in with you, even for the short-term."

"I see."

When her bottom lip trembled, he felt like a jerk and a bully. She looked small and defenseless in the big bed, though he knew that was only an illusion.

He sighed. "I don't want to hurt you." Hell, he didn't want to hurt himself.

She smiled, though her eyes glistened with tears. "I can handle honesty, Dr. Hutchinson. Let me get my stomach under control, and after that I doubt our paths will cross very often."

It didn't take a medical degree to know when a woman was hurt and fighting back. Rolling to his feet, he straightened the covers on his side of the bed. There was probably some kind of comment that would smooth this situation, but he hadn't a clue what it was.

"Do you want to try some water again?" he asked.

"Absolutely not." She shuddered.

"You'll have to eventually."

"Thanks, Dr. Obvious."

"I forgot what a smart mouth you have." His neck heated.

"And I forgot what a pompous, holier-than-thou hypocrite you are."

"Hypocrite? Seriously? How so?" His temper had a long, slow fuse. But Simone knew how to pour gasoline on any argument.

"You may be done with love and romance for now because Bethany broke your heart. I'll leave you to your crusty bachelorhood, believe me. But I wasn't the only one in the middle of that kiss the other day. I know when a man wants me."

"Damn it, Simone."

"Are you denying it?"

He'd taken an oath to heal and to protect. At the moment, he wanted to strangle his erstwhile patient. "Good night, brat. I'll be in to check on you several times, but use the phone if you need to. I'm close by."

She smirked at him. "Saint Hutch."

He didn't bother turning on lights in the house. During his rural rotations there had been many nights when he and his team only had enough fuel for two hours of lantern light. After that, he'd learned to maneuver in the dark under any circumstances.

He found a new toothbrush in one of the guest bathrooms. Since he always kept a change of clothes in the trunk of his car, he was able to put on a clean shirt and pants after a quick shower.

In the living room, he surveyed the sofa. Actually, it wasn't as small as Simone had intimated. If he bent his knees or propped his feet on the arm, he'd be fine. The couch was leather and cool to the touch. He settled down and pulled an afghan over his lower body.

Fatigue could be measured in degrees. There had been times in Sudan when he worked sixteen hours straight. In the blistering heat. On those nights, he had stumbled to bed and collapsed, asleep in seconds.

Now he was definitely tired. But it was different. Though his body wanted rest, his brain spun like a hamster wheel. Going nowhere.

Simone made him ache—not only physically, though that was certainly true, but emotionally, as well. If he could go back and undo the past, he would never have asked her to dance. That one misstep had led them down a narrow, treacherous road that petered out into nothing.

Time was supposed to heal all wounds. By rights, he should be able to look at his past and acknowledge that things had worked out for the best. But the opposite was true. He felt empty. Even in Africa, when he knew he was saving lives and improving the quality of other lives, he'd learned a painful truth. His being there had been a lie, in part.

Unlike Bethany, who had been so very confident and sure of herself and her life's goals, Hutch had gone to Sudan a broken man. He had utilized his training. He had contributed to the greater good. Still, it hadn't been enough.

He'd been adrift…lost. Losing Simone had made him doubt himself and his place in the world. Eventually, falling in love with Bethany had helped heal the rough places and ease his loneliness. But even before she died, he'd wondered fleetingly if he was using her as a stand-in for the woman he really wanted.

Closing his eyes, he practiced the relaxation techniques he'd used in med school. One muscle group at a time. He dozed on and off, never fully comatose. Many doctors were light sleepers, ready to spring into action when the situation demanded. Which reminded him of the real reason he was here.

He had set the alarm on his phone for three-hour intervals. At one o'clock, he walked quietly down the hall and peeked into the patient's room. If she was resting well, he didn't want to bother her. "Simone?" He whispered her name. She wouldn't hear him unless she was awake.

"Come on in." Her voice was soft, but alert.

"Why aren't you sleeping?"

"I did sleep. For a little while."

"And now?"

"I'm hungry."

"But still nauseated?"

"Oh, yeah…"

He hesitated. "Simone…"

"What?"

"I've seen acupressure really help in these situations. One of the doctors I worked with in West Darfur was Chinese. He taught me the technique, and I actually used it on half a dozen women in my care."

"Is there a downside?"

"I'd have to hold your hand for three minutes. Each one."

A long silence ensued.

Finally, Simone spoke. "Sounds pretty risqué."

He choked out a laugh and sat on the end of the bed. Even at her lowest points, Simone was still able to manufacture humor. That ability boded well for a difficult pregnancy.

"Well," he said, "what do you think?"

"I'd dance with the devil if I thought it would make me feel better."

"Gee, thanks," he said drily. "Your enthusiasm is duly noted."

He stood up and moved closer. "We can do this with you sitting up or lying down, whichever feels the most comfortable." The bizarre situation somehow seemed more acceptable, because it was the middle of the night.

"I'll stay put," she said. "Don't want to make any sudden moves that might tip the balance."

It made more sense to sit on the bed, but instead he grabbed the small chair from the vanity and positioned it at Simone's elbow. He wanted the illusion of distance. For the same reason, he didn't turn on the lamp. The faint illumination from the night-light in the bathroom was all he needed.

Most of this procedure was by touch, anyway. He had learned where to apply pressure. It wasn't an exact science, but he had practiced enough to feel comfortable doing it.

Now if he could be equally at ease with his beautiful guinea pig, he might come out of this next half hour unscathed. "Let's do the easiest one first," he said. Her left hand rested at the edge of the mattress. He picked up her arm, noting that her fingers were cold.

"Will it hurt?" she asked.

He had a hunch that the nervous question was more about him touching her than any real fear of acupressure. "It shouldn't. But if I press too hard, tell me."

Over the years, he had learned that speaking to a patient in steady, reassuring tones while in the midst of a difficult or painful procedure was helpful. In Simone's case, the distraction might prove useful for *both* of them.

Turning her hand palm up, he pressed his thumb to her soft skin. "The spot for this is P6," he said. "About three fingers above the crease of your wrist and in between two tendons." He applied pressure. "Okay so far?"

She nodded.

Three minutes was a hell of a long time when a man held a woman in a dark bedroom and knew every one of the reasons he couldn't or wouldn't let himself be drawn in again. He counted off the seconds in his head, trying to ignore the fact that she trembled.

After an eternity, he cleared his throat. "Other hand," he said.

He hoped this was going to help, because it was tearing him apart. Her hair fanned out across the pillow. The thin, silky nightgown she wore was cut low in the front. Though at first she clutched the sheet in a death grip, when she shifted slightly and gave him her right arm, he could see the shadow of her cleavage and the outline of her breasts.

God help him. He kept the pressure firm, resisting the urge to stroke upward to the crease of her elbow.

Kissing her there had been a game he played in the past, a teasing caress she always swore tickled. But it also made her sigh and melt into his embrace.

"Hasn't it been long enough?"

Simone's timid question snapped him out of his reverie. He'd lost count of the seconds. "I think so," he muttered. He released her and sat back. "How do you feel?"

She rubbed her wrists together and flexed her fingers. "Better. I think. Is this honestly a valid treatment?"

"Been around for thousands of years."

"I hesitate to tempt fate, but I think I could eat something."

"Good. That's usually the case. The effects aren't permanent, of course, but you can take advantage in the interim. What can I get for you?"

"Let's start small. Dry toast with a tiny bit of apple jelly? Do you mind?"

"Of course not."

In the kitchen, he rested his forehead against the cool stainless steel of the refrigerator door. This wasn't going to work. He'd find someone else to help out, but it couldn't be him.

Desire was a steady ache in his gut. And it wasn't even entirely about sex. He wanted to crawl into that bed and hold her. Too many nights in the last few years he had summoned Simone's image to get through the hot, lonely hours. He'd missed home. He had missed his friends and colleagues. He had even missed the unpredictable Texas weather.

Now he had returned home, and almost everything was back to normal. Almost, but not quite.

On autopilot, he retrieved the bread and prepared a single piece of toast. Simone had to start slow. Her stomach had suffered significant trauma in the past few days.

In the end, he was gone maybe twenty minutes. When he returned, she was sitting up. He frowned. "You should have let me help you."

Simone's smile was sunny. "I think I can eat," she said. "You're a miracle worker, Dr. Hutchinson."

"Don't get too excited," he cautioned. "The nausea will likely come back."

"I can handle that," she said. "At least if I can have some normalcy in between."

He offered her the small plate. "One bite at a time. We're in no rush."

She nodded. Carefully, she took one dainty bite. Clearly, she was so excited about eating that she had forgotten her state of dress. He tried not to stare. Instead, he prowled her bedroom, studying the things with which she had surrounded herself.

Between two large windows, a tall set of antique barrister bookshelves held a collection of travel books, popular novels and childhood favorites. In another corner, an overstuffed armchair and matching ottoman provided a cozy reading spot. Books were only one of many passions he and Simone had shared.

He remembered a summer picnic in the country long ago when they had laughed and enjoyed playful sex and finally rested in the shade of a giant oak. While he had drowsed with his head in Simone's lap, she had read aloud to him from a book of poetry. That might have been the moment he knew he was in love with her. She was so much more than a beauti-

ful woman or a wealthy debutante or a Texas Cattleman's Club darling.

Simone Parker was a free spirit, a lover of life. She
was warm and intelligent and effortlessly charming.
Other men had looked at him with envious eyes when
he and Simone were out together in public. She was
the kind of woman some guys considered a trophy
girlfriend.

To Hutch, she had simply been his life. When they
met, he'd been twenty-eight. Plenty old enough to have
sown his proverbial wild oats. About the time he'd
been rethinking his plans to head off to Africa, Simone had cut him loose. She'd insisted that he was a
gifted doctor and that she wouldn't stand in his way.

"Hutch!"

Pushing the painful thoughts away, he spun around,
alarmed. "What is it?"

Simone beamed. "I ate it. And I think it's going to
stay down. Will you pour me some water?"

He did so immediately and handed her the glass.
"Tiny sips," he cautioned.

She scrunched up her face as she drank the water
one tablespoon at a time. "That's enough," she said
finally.

"How do you feel?"

"Tired. Weird. But not pregnant. Is that bad?" She
bit her bottom lip, a telltale sign she was agitated.

He took the glass and set it back on the table. "Of
course not. It will be a long time before you start to
show, especially because you've lost weight already.
As far as actually feeling the babies kick, I'd guess
that will be weeks from now. So it's no surprise you

don't feel pregnant. That's why Mother Nature gives you three trimesters to get used to the idea."

"I suppose…"

"Can you go back to sleep now?"

She slid back down in the bed and straightened the covers. "I think so."

"And the nausea?"

"Hardly any right now. Thank you, Hutch."

He shrugged. "I'm glad the acupressure worked. Sometimes modern medicine looks for answers when they're right at hand."

"Right at hand." She giggled. "Dr. Hutch made a funny. Get it? You held my hands?"

"If I didn't know better, I'd think you'd been drinking," he said ruefully.

"I would never do anything so foolish. I'm just giddy with relief that you made the nausea go away, even for an hour. Are there other people in Royal who might know how to do what you did?"

The intent behind her question was obvious. Neither of them thought Hutch should be the one to help her through the terrible sickness produced by her pregnancy. Nevertheless, he spoke the truth. "I doubt it, Simone. Maybe in one of the big cities. But Royal is not exactly a hotbed of ancient Asian medical practice."

"I see."

It was impossible to miss the layers of frustration and unease she gave off. "We'll figure something out," he promised. "One day at a time."

She moved restlessly. "I shouldn't have let you kiss me the other day. That was wrong of me. I'm sorry."

"Forget about it. I could have stopped."

"Why didn't you?" she asked softly.

It was a very good question. One he had asked himself a dozen times since. He was a grown-ass man. He knew better than to show weakness to Simone.

"I guess part of me wanted to remember," he muttered. "But now all I want to do is forget."

Six

When Simone awoke next, she realized she had slept for six hours straight. Her head was clear, and although she did indeed feel sick again, it wasn't at the intense level she had experienced recently.

As she stretched and tried to convince herself she could get up and go to the bathroom without incident, a woman in navy scrubs peeked her head around the door. "Ms. Parker? Good, you're awake. I'm Barb Kellum. Dr. Hutchinson called me and said you needed some help."

"That would be great," Simone said. "I'd love to get a shower."

The nurse smiled. "First things first, young lady. Let's eat a bit of breakfast and go from there. I brought over some of my homemade chicken broth. Warmed it in the microwave. How does that sound?"

The nurse with the salt-and-pepper hair was mid-fiftyish, tall and sturdily built. Her eyes were kind, but her tone of voice was more drill sergeant than nanny.

Simone smiled hesitantly. "I'll give it a try. But I make no promises."

While Simone sat up in bed, the nurse bustled about, straightening the covers and carefully placing a white wooden tray over Simone's lap. The serving piece must have come with Barb as well, because Simone had never seen it. Although the china, glass and silverware were arranged artistically, Simone's stomach rebelled at the aroma of the chicken broth.

Barbara picked up the bowl and held it under Simone's nose. "Don't let your brain overrule your stomach. You're hungry, even if you don't know it. Breathe in and tell yourself you're about to have a treat."

Amazingly, it worked. Mostly. Inhaling the scent of the thin soup sent a sharp hunger pang through Simone's stomach. She picked up the spoon and scooped up the first bite. "What if this doesn't work?"

Barbara pointed at the floor beside the bed. "Basin and plastic ready. Nothing to worry about."

It took half an hour, but Simone finished every spoonful. Afterward, she scooted down onto the mattress and lay there frozen, afraid to move. "How long before you think it's safe to get up?"

The nurse shook her head. "Sorry, love, but you can't play that game. It might help the nausea, but your muscles will start to atrophy if we don't keep you on your feet. Exercise can actually help nausea."

The following few hours were a lesson in patience. Barb unhooked the IV and hovered as Simone visited the bathroom. After that, the two of them managed a modified shower for Simone. She threw up twice in the process, but it wasn't as violent as the episodes earlier in the week.

Once she was clean and dry, she felt as weak as a baby.

Barb beamed at her. "I'd say we did well, Ms. Parker."

"Please call me Simone."

"And I answer to Barb. Now sit in that chair for half a shake while I remake the bed. Nothing feels better after a shower than clean sheets."

By the time Simone was tucked back into bed and the IV was reattached, she felt embarrassingly exhausted. "How long do I have to be hooked up?"

Barbara checked her blood pressure and pulse before answering. "That all depends on how much you can eat on your own. I'll draw blood after lunch and send it off to the lab. Then again before dinner. Tomorrow, Dr. Hutchinson will read the results and assess how you're doing."

The nurse was right about clean sheets. Simone's eyes were heavy. "Is it okay if I nap?"

"Definitely. Later, we'll try a walk around the house. Don't worry, Ms. Parker. You'll survive this, I promise."

Simone dozed on and off during the next hour, watching the patterns of light and shadow on the ceiling. All her problems hovered just offstage, but for now, she was content to drift. She vaguely remembered Hutch checking on her a couple of times last night after the acupressure incident, but they hadn't spoken since. Beneath the sheet, she laced her fingers over her abdomen. Her stomach was flat and smooth, the muscles taut and firm. Though she had friends and acquaintances who had already become mothers, she had never thought much about the process. At least not until her grandfather died.

Suddenly, she realized she hadn't looked at her email in over forty-eight hours. Stealthily, not wanting to incur Barb's wrath, she reached into the bottom drawer of the bedside table and retrieved her laptop. Leaning on one elbow, she opened it up and turned it on. Fortunately, her battery charge was at 50 percent. She could do a few things quickly without asking for help.

Email was not a problem. She deleted the junk and replied to a couple of queries that needed an immediate answer. Then, with shaky fingers, she logged on to Facebook and checked the message box. A tiny numeral one appeared on the icon. Damn. Most of her friends texted her. The only recent Facebook message she had received was one from the mysterious Maverick. Maverick—the anonymous, eerie, dark presence who had threatened many of the citizens of Royal, one after another.

Simone's first message had appeared two weeks ago. Since nothing bad had happened in the interim, she'd hoped the blackmailer had moved on to someone else. Apparently not.

The message was brief and vindictive.

Simone Parker, you're a money-grubbing bitch. Enjoy life now, because soon everyone in town will know what you have done and why. Maverick.

She shut the computer quickly and tucked it under a pillow. This time, the nausea roiling in her belly had more to do with fear and disgust than it did with pregnancy. All she could think about was the look on Hutch's face if he ever learned the truth.

Unfortunately, Barb returned about that time and frowned. "You're flushed. What's wrong?"

Simone didn't bother answering. She was afraid she would cry. The thought that someone in Royal hated her enough to blackmail her was distressing. She wasn't a saint—far from it. But she tried to learn from her mistakes.

The nurse took her pulse and frowned. "You need to calm down, young lady. Stress isn't good for the babies. What brought this on?"

Simone scrambled for a convincing lie. "I have so much to do at work. Each day I get farther behind. I need to make plans...to decide how I'll manage three babies. It's a lot, you know."

Barb nodded sympathetically. "I understand, I do. But you can't climb a mountain in bare feet. Baby steps, remember. First we have to get you stabilized and healthy. Then you'll have plenty of time to plan for the future."

"Easy for you to say," Simone muttered in a whisper. Did no one understand what a colossal mess she had made of her life? It wasn't as if she could wave a magic wand and get a do-over.

Lunch was not as successful as breakfast. Two bites of lemon gelatin came right back up. But Simone waited an hour and tried again with better results. Afterward, Barb brought in her tray of torture implements. Having blood drawn was no fun, but Simone knew she had to get used to it.

Next was another nap, and after that, Barb came in to say it was time for a walk around the house. Simone leaned on the older woman unashamedly as they made a circuit from room to room. Clearly, this was necessary, because already her muscles were quivering.

Finally, she was allowed to collapse into bed again. Meanwhile, Barb changed out the IV bag, straightened the room and drew more blood. As she packed up the vials, she eyed Simone with an assessing gaze. "Will you be okay for the next few hours? I hate to leave you alone, but I promised a friend I'd sit with her mother at the nursing home this evening."

"I'll be fine," Simone said. "Dr. Hutchinson showed me how to unhook things so I can go the bathroom, and I'm feeling much stronger. Don't worry about me."

"There's more gelatin and broth in the fridge. And I brought you a fresh box of saltines this morning."

"You've been wonderful. Will you be here tomorrow?"

Barb nodded. "Dr. Hutchinson said at least three days."

"Okay then. I'll see you in the morning."

"Should I bring the meal before I go?"

"It's still early. I'd rather wait."

"All right then." She gave a little wave. "I'll let myself out."

With the nurse gone and Hutch still presumably at the hospital, the house was desperately quiet. As the sunlight faded, Simone felt the weight of her situation drag her down. Whatever lay ahead, she would take care of these innocent babies. If she decided she was incapable of functioning as a single mother, she could give them up for adoption when they were born. There were likely dozens of couples in Royal with fertility issues who would be overjoyed at the chance to give three little babies a home.

The thought left Simone feeling hollow. Not only had she rushed into this situation with less than pure motives, she had given little or no thought to the future. Now that she was pregnant, the situation was painfully real.

At six thirty, she actually felt hungry…in a normal way. Hutch had said he'd be back, but who knew what kind of emergencies might have come up.

Mindful of her promises to Barb, she sat on the side of the bed for a full three minutes before attempting to get up. Unhooking the IV was not hard once she'd learned what to do. Walking slowly, she made her way to the kitchen and opened the refrigerator. After eating a few bites of the gelatin, she drank half a glass of ginger ale. The calories she had consumed today were helping. She felt steadier and stronger already.

Darkness closed in, and with it, her uneasiness returned. Hutch had given her his phone number. Should she simply text him and tell him not to come?

When she saw headlights flash as a car turned into her driveway, she scurried back to the bedroom, reattached the IV and settled into bed. She didn't want Hutch to think she was being reckless. It was important to her that he knew she was taking this pregnancy seriously.

When he finally appeared at her door, he looked tired, but wonderful.

"Hey there," he said, his lips curving in a half smile. "Barb said you had a pretty good day."

Simone nodded. "I'd give it a seven and a half. Thank you for suggesting her. She's very kind and competent."

"How's your stomach?" He sat on the foot of the bed and ran his hands over his face. He had obviously showered before leaving the hospital, because he smelled like the outdoors, all fresh and masculine.

She sat up and scooped her hair away from her face. Barb had taken the time to blow-dry it after Simone's shower. Now it fell straight and silky around her shoulders. "We're on speaking terms again. Barely."

"Good."

"Have *you* eaten?"

"I grabbed a burger in the cafeteria."

"That's not entirely healthy. Physician, heal thyself."

"You let me worry about me. What did you have for dinner?"

"Some gelatin. I was contemplating Barb's homemade chicken broth, but I'm feeling pretty normal at the moment, and I'd hate to tempt fate."

"You look better."

His steady regard made her blush. "Thank you."

"How 'bout I warm the broth and bring it to you?"

"Okay," she said reluctantly. "If you insist."

Hutch grinned. "I do."

While he was gone, she grabbed a small mirror out of her purse and examined her reflection. Other than having cheekbones that were too sharp, she didn't look half bad. Pinching her cheeks added color to her face.

Hutch must have found the bed tray in the kitchen.

When he returned with her modest meal, he had poured a serving of broth into a crockery bowl and added a glass of ice water, along with some soda crackers.

Simone scooted up in bed. "Barb is a good cook."

"Her specialty is invalid food."

She wrinkled her nose. "That's a terrible way to describe it."

"Sorry."

The stilted conversation was awkward, to say the least. "You don't have to watch me eat, Hutch. And you don't need to spend the night. I'm much better. I appreciate all you've done."

He shrugged, his expression impassive. "One more night won't hurt. I'll have the results of your blood work in the morning. If everything looks sound, you can follow up next week with Dr. Fetter at a regular appointment."

"And you'll ride off into the sunset to rescue another damsel in distress."

His eyes narrowed. His jaw tightened. "Are you pissed that I went to Africa? Is that it, Simone? If you'll recall, I offered to stay here until you got your agency off the ground. But you were pretty emphatic that I should go. So don't blame me for the mess you've made of your life."

She swallowed hard. Already, her stomach cramped with nerves and nausea, and she hadn't even taken a bite yet. The old Hutch would never have been so blunt. There was a time he'd humored her every whim and thought her biting sarcasm was funny.

Not so much anymore.

She lifted her chin, striving for dignity. "You're

right. I apologize. Now if you don't mind, I think I'll have a better chance of getting this to go down successfully if I don't have an audience. And to be clear, I don't blame you for anything. You're an easy target, and I'm at the end of my rope. But don't worry, Hutch. I'll be just fine."

Hutch cursed softly, striding rapidly out of the room. How was it possible for one small woman to make him feel like a complete and utter failure? No one in his entire adult life had caused him as many sleepless nights as Simone Parker. Not even Bethany.

He prowled the house, pacing from room to room, feeling his bitterness and frustration grow. Though he finally managed to sleep for a few hours, at 3:00 a.m. he was up again. In the darkest moments of the night, he at last admitted to himself why he was so angry.

In some foolish, illogical corner of his brain, he had entertained the hope that he and Simone might mend fences. Despite his utter despair at losing Bethany, seeing Simone that first day in the exam room at the hospital had given him hope.

But the feeling was a lie. He was a bloody idiot. He and Simone were no more compatible than they had ever been. She had a chip on her shoulder so big it was a wonder it didn't crush her. Surely she didn't expect him to sit at her feet like a puppy dog begging for scraps. Those babies she carried weren't his. She didn't want to be married. Not to him, not to anyone. With this unconventional pregnancy, she was thumbing her nose at the world.

He might not understand why, but he knew it was true.

At last, sheer exhaustion trumped his fury. He went

to Simone's bedroom to check the IV, more for something to do than any real expectation that the bag was empty. Barb had changed it late that afternoon.

What he heard as he stood in the hallway put a knot in his chest.

Simone was crying...not just crying, but sobbing. Plucky, confident, decisive Simone sounded as if her heart was completely broken.

He backed away quietly, not wanting to embarrass her. Then he stopped. Not even the most coldhearted of bastards could leave her in that condition.

Though he suffered misgivings on a massive scale, he padded over to the bed in his sock feet and crouched beside her. She lay on her back with one arm flung over her eyes.

"Simone," he whispered, not wanting to alarm her. "Stop crying, honey. It only makes things worse."

Without waiting for permission, he unhooked the IV, scooped her up and sat down with her in his lap. Leaning against the headboard, he stroked her hair. "Talk to me, little mama. Tell me what's going on in that head of yours."

Though she huffed and protested and struggled briefly, he felt the moment she went limp in his embrace. She burrowed into his chest like a frightened child. Tears wet his shirt. The sobs were less ferocious, but the crying didn't stop.

It worried him. Simone was not one to give up on any challenge. He'd never seen her like this. Gently, he held her close, telling himself the position was for her benefit. He didn't even flinch at the lie. That's how easy it was for his libido to seize the wheel.

Minutes ticked away on the clock. Simone was a

welcome weight against his body. Though she was too thin, and arguably not at her best, to him, she was as stunningly beautiful as she had ever been. Imagining her round belly in the advanced stages of pregnancy flooded him with an entirely inappropriate rush of arousal.

At one time, he had envisioned that scenario with pride and anticipation. Now everything was wrong. And he felt powerless to make it right.

Seven

"Enough, Simone," he said firmly. "That's enough."

Gradually, she calmed. Except for the occasional tiny, hiccupping sob, the storm was over.

He played with her hair, plaiting it between his fingers. He didn't touch her breasts. He wanted to… God knows he wanted to. But that would be too much temptation. He wasn't prepared to throw all caution to the wind.

Pregnancy was the most natural thing in the world, and yet complicated. From teenagers who didn't mean to get pregnant to full-grown women who craved a child and couldn't conceive, the process was messy and fraught with pitfalls. He couldn't imagine the toll this was taking on Simone emotionally.

He smoothed his palm over her back. "Better now?" he asked.

She nodded, sitting up and sniffling. Her damp eyes were sapphires framed in coal-black lashes. "Hutch."

His name was a caress on her lips, a sweet, irresistible invitation. God help him. He slid his hands beneath her hair and steadied her head, tipping her mouth up for his kiss. He wanted her to stop him. He needed her to be alarmed and outraged. Instead, she leaned into him.

Their lips clung, mated. She tasted like toothpaste. "Sweet Simone," he muttered, easing her onto her back. He moved half on top of her, his leg wedged between her thighs. She sighed and welcomed him, though her thin nightgown hampered her movements.

He kissed her forehead, her eyelids, her slender throat. Simone arched against him, her breathing ragged. When he made his way down to the place where the neckline of her gown covered her breasts, Simone stiffened for the first time.

Instinctively, he drew back. He was half out of his mind, but not so far gone he didn't know when a woman said no. Verbal or body language, it didn't matter.

She frowned. "Why did you stop?"

"I felt you tense up."

"Not because of you."

"Then why?"

"I don't want to hurt the babies."

He smiled, though it took an effort. "Nothing a man and a woman do in this situation is cause for alarm. I swear to you."

She kept one hand on his shoulder, the other free to comb through his hair. The feel of her fingertips on his scalp made him shiver. "Hutch?"

"Yes?"

"I guess it's obvious we both need this. But it won't mean anything beyond tonight. It can't."

"Is that an ultimatum?" Why couldn't the damn woman live in the moment? That was a lesson he had learned in Sudan when life was so very fragile and joy came only in fleeting snatches.

She rubbed her thumb across his cheekbone. "No ultimatum." She sighed.

"Do you want me?"

"So much it hurts. Is that normal?"

"Many pregnant women find themselves with increased libido."

Simone laughed at him. "You're funny when you get all serious and medical."

"Most people respect my position and my expertise."

"Most people haven't seen you naked."

His lips twisted in a wry grin. He would never develop too much of an inflated ego with Simone around. "Are you feeling ill? At all?"

She wrapped one slender, toned thigh around his leg. "I'm good to go."

Hutch knew he was making a mistake. Simone must have known it, too. But the heat and yearning between them was too powerful to ignore. "I've been tested recently," he said. "I'm clean."

"I'm in the clear also. And it's not like you're going to knock me up." The line should have been funny, but neither of them laughed.

Very deliberately—to give them both a chance to change their minds—he stood and stripped off his clothes. Simone tracked his every move. Afterward, he helped her sit up, and they both managed to raise her gown over her head. She wasn't wearing any underwear, so now she was completely nude.

He reclined beside her and put a tentative hand on her belly. "Odd, isn't it…that you can't really feel anything when so much is going on?"

She leaned against him, her hand on top of his. "I'm scared, Hutch."

"Of which part?" He kissed her softly, almost lightheaded because every bit of blood had rushed south to his sex.

"All of it. Labor. Delivery. Bringing home three newborns. Trying to breastfeed."

"Women have been doing this since the dawn of time. You're smart and organized. I have no doubt you'll conquer motherhood like you do every other hurdle in your life."

"Make love to me, Hutch."

Her eyes were damp. She seemed more sad than amorous. But he couldn't tell her no. Not anymore.

Carefully, he spread her legs and tested her readiness with two fingers. Her sex was moist and swollen. "Simone," he groaned. He slid into her with one steady push. The sensation was indescribable. Pausing to let her adjust to his size, he rested his forehead on her shoulder. Her fingernails scored his back.

"More," she demanded. "More, Hutch."

He lost his mind. There was no other way to describe it. His fantasies from endless dark, hot, uncomfortable nights in West Darfur burst into life with a euphoric explosion that took him to the brink of a powerful orgasm in seconds. He could tell Simone wasn't far behind.

Deliberately, he reached between their sweat-slickened bodies and found the little spot that made her tumble over the edge. They clung to each other like survivors in the aftermath of a killer wave.

The room was dark and silent. At last, he pushed up onto one elbow and cupped her cheek with his hand. "Again?" he asked hoarsely.

"Yes," she whispered. "Again…"

Simone spent the waning hours of the night wrapped in Hutch's arms. He spooned her, her back pressed to his chest. Though she felt his sex flex against her bottom, stiff and ready, they didn't make love again.

It was the most restful sleep she'd experienced in the last two weeks. If she tried really hard, she could pretend the past five years never happened.

Toward morning, the nausea returned. Hutch held her hair and washed her face after she retched helplessly. He helped put her nightgown back on and sat with her, coaxing her bite by bite until she finished several crackers.

Then Barb arrived and Hutch transformed into Dr. Hutchinson. "I'll call with the lab results," he said, his expression distant and remote.

"Thank you," Simone said, her heart shredding in agony.

Barb bustled about, oblivious to the tension in the room.

Hutch nodded. "You ladies have a good day. I need to get to the hospital."

When Simone didn't reply, he spun on his heel and walked out.

After that, the day was an endurance test. Eat. Get

sick. Eat again. But the episodes were coming further apart, and she was actually managing to keep food down long enough to reap the benefits.

When Hutch called the landline with Simone's test results, Barb answered and jotted down some numbers. She hung up the phone and gave Simone a thumbs-up. "Your electrolytes and other blood levels are right where they need to be, young lady. Let's take that needle out of your hand and allow you to get back to normal."

Barb stayed for the remainder of the day, but it was clear that Simone was learning to manage the nausea on her own. The efficient nurse said her good-byes just before five o'clock, about the time Cecelia showed up with a huge pan of lasagna and a crusty loaf of French bread.

Cecelia blanched when Simone got teary-eyed. "What did I do?" she asked urgently. "Are you in pain?"

Simone hugged her tightly. "I'm just so glad to see you."

Her beautiful blonde friend carried everything through to the kitchen. "No garlic on the bread and no heavy spices in the lasagna. I'm determined to fatten you up. You look awful, hon."

Simone simply shook her head. Was there no one who would lie to her and tell her she looked great? "I feel like I could eat the whole pan. But I won't," she said hastily. "My poor stomach is barely speaking to me as it is."

Cecelia nodded. "It should keep in the fridge for several days. When will you be able to go back to work?"

"I know you're worried about your campaign, but

I'm not going to drop the ball, I promise. I'm planning to go in tomorrow, even if I have to cut the day short."

The other woman raised one perfect eyebrow. "Please give me some credit. I'm not worried about the campaign, I'm worried about *you*, Simone. Would you mind telling me why in the world you had to get pregnant right now? It doesn't make sense."

"I thought Naomi filled you in." Simone perched on a stool at the granite counter. She didn't really want to go through the whole explanation again, especially when it wasn't all that believable the first time.

Cecelia waved a hand, the one not showcasing her amazing engagement ring. "Naomi tried to put a positive spin on it, but I wasn't buying it. Since when do *you* want to be a mother?"

Cecelia's skepticism stung. "Is that really so hard to imagine?"

"You've poured your heart and soul into the agency. You've dated one or two…not more than three guys since Hutch headed off to Africa. And never once have you given any indication that your biological clock is ticking any louder than mine or Naomi's. I know you, girl. Something strange is going on." Cecelia broke off a warm piece of bread, wrapped it in a paper napkin and handed it to Simone. "Tell Auntie Cee Cee what's up, or I'll be forced to resort to blackmail."

It was a poor choice of words. When Simone flinched, Cecelia frowned. "What did I say? You know I was only kidding. But seriously, Simone. Tell me what the heck is going on."

Sooner or later the truth would come out. Sooner or later Simone would have to confide in her two best friends. But she still felt raw and guilty about her decision. She needed time to come to terms with what she had done before she came clean completely.

"It's true," she muttered. "There's more to this than you know. I won't keep it a secret forever. But in the meantime, I need you to be my friend and tell me everything is going to work out fine."

"Is that because the gorgeous doctor is going to step in and make an honest woman out of you?"

"Don't even joke about that," Simone snapped. "Hutch doesn't deserve to be dragged into my mess."

"Well, maybe he'll at least stick around this time." Cecelia's dour comment made Simone want to rush to Hutch's defense. The man had simply followed his dreams and his calling. While she appreciated her friend's wholehearted support, it really wasn't fair to paint Hutch as the villain.

"Let's eat," Simone said. "The lasagna smells amazing. And if you don't mind, let's not talk about Hutch or babies or my sordid secrets. Dr. Fetter says stress can make my nausea worse."

"Sordid?" Cecelia perked up. "I'm intrigued."

"You're also wildly happy, aren't you?" Simone said, trying to change the subject as she piled a small dollop of lasagna on her plate. "Deacon must be good for you. I'm pretty sure you're glowing."

Cecelia's smile was smug. "He's amazing. And we're both thrilled about the baby."

"I'm very happy for you."

Cecelia sobered for a moment. "Is it true you're having triplets?"

Simone nodded. "As long as nothing goes wrong. Sometimes one fetus doesn't develop. It's too soon to know."

"Would you be relieved if you only had one or two?"

Trust Cecelia to cut to the heart of the matter. "You'd think so, wouldn't you? Lord knows how I'll manage. But now that I know there are three, I want them all so badly. It doesn't make any sense. I can't really explain it. All I know is that I would be heartbroken if anything happened to even one of them. I feel like their mother already."

Cecelia leaned over to hug her. "I get it, hon. This whole pregnancy thing turns the world upside down." She hesitated, clearly looking for a tactful way to phrase her question. "So how does the good doctor figure into all of this? Naomi said he was here the other night when she came over."

"He's the new head of the maternal-fetal department at the hospital. Not *my* doctor," Simone said hastily. "I'm Dr. Fetter's patient. But I'm considered high-risk because of the multiples. Hutch oversees and keep tabs on all the cases."

"And does he make house calls to each of those pregnant women?"

"Of course not."

Cecelia rolled her eyes. "Fine. Live in the land of denial while you can."

Simone felt her face get hot. What would Cecelia and Naomi think if they knew about last night? "I doubt I'll see much of him. The only reason he was here is that I chose to have my IV at home instead of taking up a hospital bed. He wanted to make sure I was okay. That's all."

"Whatever you say, little chick. I won't harass you when you're so sick. Still, the day of reckoning will come. Don't think you can avoid this subject forever."

That was the problem, Simone thought bleakly. With this Maverick person threatening her, she was always going to have the sword of Damocles hanging over her head. Telling her parents was going to be bad. She knew she had to do it soon. If they got wind of her pregnancy any other way, they might pressure her into marrying the baby's father. How was she going to explain that the mystery man was no more to her than a control number on a test tube?

Cecelia waved a hand in front of Simone's face. "Hello, in there. Anybody home?"

Simone took a bite of lasagna and washed it down with tea. "Sorry. I was thinking."

"About what?" Cecelia said. Clearly, *her* pregnancy was going well. She ate an astonishing amount of lasagna with no consequences as far as Simone could see.

"I don't want to make a big deal about this pregnancy. Especially not this early, not when there's a chance I could miscarry."

"Lots of people wait until after the first trimester to make any kind of announcement."

"True. But you know how gossip flies in this town. The fact that I was taken from my office on a stretcher is not a secret."

"You'll figure something out," Cecelia said breezily. She grabbed her sweater and purse. "I've gotta run. I'm meeting Deacon for a late dessert."

"Oh, Cecelia. Why didn't you tell me? You should have dropped off the lasagna and had dinner with your brand-new fiancé."

Cecelia's grin was cheeky. "Don't be silly. That lucky man gets to eat dinner with me the rest of his life. He won't begrudge me one evening with a sick friend."

"I'm doing better, honestly."

"Good. 'Cause to tell you the truth, Naomi had me worried after she saw you the other night."

"Let her know I'm fine."

"I will." Cecelia hugged her. "I'll call you tomorrow. Don't worry about the campaign. You're the most important thing to me. Love you, hon."

And with that, Simone's gorgeous friend blew out the door.

Simone stood at the living room window and watched the car fly down the driveway and onto the main road. Suddenly, she was aware of the crushing silence in the house. No Cecelia or Naomi. No Barb. No Hutch.

He had talked about staying three nights, but she was better now. All her tests had come back with good results. The nurse had removed the IV and packed up all the paraphernalia to take back to the hospital. There was absolutely no reason for Hutch to return.

Life was back to normal. Almost.

Telling herself she wasn't depressed, Simone took a shower and changed into an old pair of yoga pants and an oversize T-shirt. She'd spent far too much time in bed. She wanted to get outside and breathe the fresh spring air.

Not bothering to put on shoes, she opened the back door and made her way down the steps. Dr. Fetter had said moderate exercise was helpful, so Simone had no qualms about risking the babies. The healthier she was, the healthier they were.

Outside, she perked up instantly. Her gardener was

a genius. Flowers and ornamental shrubs and fruit trees met and mingled in a display that was appealing without being too formal. In the center of it all lay a deep, verdant lawn. It reminded her of the quad at college where this time of year she and her friends would toss Frisbees and sunbathe and study when they absolutely had to…

All of that seemed like a lifetime ago.

The evening air was cooler than usual. She wrapped her arms around her waist and meandered aimlessly. There in the corner might be a good spot for a play structure. Swings and a slide and maybe even a tiny house with real windows and miniature furniture inside.

It was fun to daydream, because she wanted to be a good mother. She wanted her children to grow up feeling loved and supported. If she had a boy who aspired to be a ballet dancer or a girl who loved fire engines, she would nurture them and help them follow their dreams.

But what happened when the babies grew old enough to ask about their father? What would she say? Stricken by her own selfishness and shortsightedness, she fell to her knees and covered her face with her hands. The scope and ramifications of her mistake were crushing. How could she ever make this right?

She blamed the cry fest on hormones. The tears leaked between her fingers and spotted the front of her shirt. In the spacious yard surrounded by a tall privacy fence, she faced the enormity of what she had done. There was no one to see her break down…no one to witness the moment she hit bottom.

Later, she wasn't sure how long she'd been kneeling there in the grass. She only knew that her knees were sore and her skin covered in gooseflesh when a very familiar voice said her name.

"Simone?"

Eight

Hutch hadn't meant to come. He'd had a hell of a long day. He was exhausted, and he needed seven or eight straight hours of uninterrupted sleep.

Despite all that, here he was at Simone's house. Again.

He crouched beside her in the grass, touching her shoulder briefly. "What's wrong, Simone? Are you hurt?" Her hair shielded her expression.

She jumped to her feet and backed away from him, rubbing the tears from her face with two hands. Her smile didn't reach her eyes. "Hormones," she said lightly. "You should know all about that. Crazy pregnant women."

After last night, he'd wondered if Simone might want more from him than medical advice. Apparently not.

He took a moment to absorb the breath-stealing

realization that she was not happy to see him. Her response was painful and unexpected. It was just as well. Hadn't he come tonight for the express purpose of telling her there was nothing between them? He wasn't prepared to risk his heart a third time. He had an important new job and little opportunity for a social life, much less a love affair.

"Barb told me you're improving slightly," he said.

"Yes. Especially in the evenings. Cecelia brought me lasagna. I managed some of that. And bread."

"Good." Fourteen hours ago they had been naked together in her bed. Now she could barely look at him. "I won't stay tonight," he said. It was a statement, but it came out sounding like a question. Would she ask him to change his mind?

"I know," she said, her gaze wary. "No need."

He cursed beneath his breath. She was far too pale. "Simone, I—"

She held up her hand. "I think we both know what last night was," she said. "Curiosity. Echoes of the past. Let's not beat ourselves up over it. Even if you wanted a repeat, I would have to say no. I need to start planning for my new family. If I hang around with you, the temptation will always be there to lean on you for help. I can't afford to do that."

"Everybody needs a hand at times."

"You know what I mean."

He did. All too well. She was putting up walls. Shutting him out.

He should be relieved. "If you go back to work, please pace yourself. Otherwise, you'll wind up in the same situation as before."

"I understand. You can trust me, Hutch. I want

these babies to be safe and healthy. I won't be stupid, I promise."

He nodded. "I should go."

"One more thing." She seemed to hesitate, as if searching for the right words. "I appreciate all you've done for me, Hutch. Later on, when I'm stronger, I'd like to make dinner for you. No strings attached," she said quickly. "Just friends."

"Okay. But you know it's not necessary."

"I want to."

"Just let me know." For some reason, he couldn't get his feet to move. "You still have my card? My phone number?" There was so much they weren't saying.

"I do." She seemed lonely and forlorn.

"Good luck, Simone."

"Thank you."

Simone watched him walk around the side of the house and disappear. The hollow feeling in her chest would get better. It had to. She was done with tears for now.

As she headed back inside, she didn't feel sleepy yet. Watching television wasn't appealing. Instead, she decided to measure one of the guest rooms. Upstairs, she had three guest rooms. The main level of the house included her master suite and a fourth guest room. That might make the best nursery.

She made a few notes and pursed her lips. How did one handle triplets? Did all three babies share? Three cribs in one space? What if one kid woke up in the middle of the night and started crying? Wouldn't that bother the other two?

Abandoning her architectural conundrum, she went

in search of the box of books Hutch had dropped by earlier in the week. She planned to start with something simple, perhaps one of the parenting guides. The medical books would be too scary. She didn't want to think about complications, even in a theoretical sense.

With a cup of decaf coffee and a cozy lap blanket, she curled up in her favorite chair in the bedroom and started to read. It wasn't only the advice about being a mom of multiples she needed, it was advice about *everything*. She felt woefully unprepared for motherhood.

At the end of a chapter, she closed the book and stared out the window. It was dark now, that time when problems grew bigger and optimism winnowed away. What would have happened if Hutch had come home a year sooner? Would she have pursued the same course? Her grandfather's death had rattled her...that and his will.

For now, the circumstances of the will were private, but Maverick seemed to know something about it. Perhaps she should go to the police. A cybercrimes expert might be able to use her laptop and trace the blackmailer's IP address.

Still, that would involve exposing her secrets, and she was scared. How would Hutch look at Simone if he learned the truth? It wasn't about the money, not really. She wanted to be recognized as a full-fledged member of the Parker family. Her father had made no secret of his disappointment that he had no son. Her grandfather had felt the same way about having only a granddaughter. Simone, as successful and ambitious as she was, was a poor substitute for two men who should have known better.

It was a skirmish she had fought her entire life. Unfortunately, in the heat of battle sometimes a person made mistakes. Simone's was a whopper. Only time would tell if she could survive the fallout.

The following morning, she made it to work more or less on time. She had set her alarm earlier than usual in order to give herself time to be sick. It was a ghastly way to start the day. Still, she counted it a victory that she had to dash to the bathroom only twice. Maybe she would be one of the lucky ones and this nausea business would eventually subside.

Her two key employees were back from the conference, so the three of them dug into the campaign for Cecelia's business. Candace must have given them some kind of report on her health, but Simone's associates were too professional and kind to grill her. Until she started showing, she hoped to be able to conceal her pregnancy and carry on as usual.

Unfortunately, even though the nausea was no longer as severe, her energy level was nonexistent. She had many, many months to go, but already these babies were impacting her life. It must have been sheer naïveté that made her think the adjustments would happen only *after* the birth.

For ten days, she had no contact with Hutch at all. Even when she visited Dr. Fetter's office at the hospital, there was no sign of the man who had returned from Africa…the man who recently shared her bed for one incredible night. Even at her lowest point, being intimate with Hutch again had made her feel like a desirable woman.

She told herself his absence from her life was for the best, and she almost believed it.

Fortunately, she was able to roll out the last of the campaign for Luna Fine Furnishings without incident and right on time. Cecelia was ecstatic. Deacon treated the three friends to dinner to celebrate. He probably enjoyed being out on the town with a trio of attractive women, but in truth, he had eyes only for Cecelia.

Simone laughed and talked during the meal, but it was hard to keep up a celebratory front. Though she was thrilled for Cecelia, it hurt to see the way Deacon looked at his bride-to-be. Simone had practically guaranteed that she would never have that kind of relationship. What kind of man would want to take on an instant family, including babies that weren't his?

She picked at her salmon, pushing the meal around on her plate so her friends would think she was eating. Unfortunately, no matter how hard she tried, she was still losing weight rather than gaining. Many pregnant women would love to have her problem, but it wasn't good for the babies.

April came to an end. May dawned with blue skies and balmy temperatures. Simone missed Hutch terribly. Knowing he was living in Royal was somehow worse than when he had been on the other side of the world.

Work became her salvation. She managed to keep her pregnancy under wraps from most of Royal, but she decided to tell her parents, come what may. She spent an uncomfortable afternoon at their house trying to explain convincingly why she'd taken the route she did.

She suspected that both her mother *and* her father knew she was going out of her way to fulfill the conditions of her grandfather's will, but they didn't press her. Perhaps her father was willing to overlook an indiscretion or poor judgment if he finally got the boy he'd always wanted.

What if all three babies were girls? What then? In that situation, Simone would have satisfied the letter of the law, but would her father still be disappointed? That would be hard to bear.

After the first few days of the month, spring began to feel like summer. The higher temperatures made Simone's nausea worse. She lived off decaf iced tea and fresh-squeezed lemonade. On the hottest days, even the mention of food was enough to make her ill.

Though she tried her best to eat, she wasn't keeping up. She grew weak and listless, and one morning she couldn't convince herself to crawl out of bed. Naomi was at a convention on the West Coast. Cecelia and Deacon had flown off to Bermuda for a quick holiday.

Simone was alone in her misery.

Around noon she knew she had to eat something. When she sat up on the side of the bed, the room spun around her. Hutch's number was programmed into her phone. All she had to do was call him.

Did he really care? Was it the doctor in him who had made the offer, or the lover? Had Simone alienated him? She never had issued the official thank-you dinner invitation, mostly because she hadn't been well enough to cook.

Stumbling to the kitchen, she held on to the walls for support. She felt terrible. This was more than simple nausea. She had a pain in her left side, and a terrible sense of foreboding. When the cramping started low in her abdomen, she panicked.

She had forgotten to bring her phone to the kitchen.

It was an agonizing trip back to the bedroom to re-
trieve it. With fumbling fingers, she found Hutch's
name and hit the call button.

One ring. Two. *Please, God, let him pick up.*

On the fourth ring, he answered. "Simone. It's nice
to hear from you." Obviously the caller ID let him
know it was her. The sound of his voice was enough
to calm her a fraction.

"I'm sorry to bother you, Hutch. Can you stop by
after work? I'm not feeling very well."

His voice sharpened. "Can you drive yourself to
the hospital?"

"No… I…" Her throat clogged with tears. "Never
mind," she whispered. "Never mind…"

Hutch heard a noise on the other end of the line as
if the phone had been dropped. His heart plummeted
to his stomach. He shoved the stack of charts he was
holding into a nearby nurse's hands and grimaced.
"I have to leave. Get Dr. Henry to cover my appoint-
ments. I'll let you know when I'll be back."

"Is everything okay, Doctor?"

"I don't know," he said grimly.

He jumped in his car and headed across town. On
the way, he called Janine Fetter and explained the situation. Today was her day off. Fortunately, they were
old friends. She agreed to meet him at Simone's house.

Hutch arrived first by minutes only. Simone always
hid her extra key in the same place, even at a new address. He tipped over the flowerpot, retrieved the key
and burst through the door, leaving it ajar for Janine.

The steps from the front door to Simone's bedroom
seemed to happen in slow motion. He found her in a

heap on the carpet, her face ashen. Her pulse was sluggish. She was clammy and barely responsive.

"Simone!" He said her name sharply, trying to cut through the fog.

Her eyelids fluttered. "Hutch? You came?"

"Of course I did," he said, cradling her in his arms. "Why are you so damned hardheaded?"

Janine arrived right about then and assessed the situation in a glance. Hutch didn't even care. The other doctor smiled at him gently. "Put her in bed and I'll examine her. You wait in the other room."

He bristled. "But I—"

She touched his arm lightly, with sympathy in her eyes. "I don't think you can be impartial about this one. Let me see what's going on. You need to take a few minutes to pull yourself together. Are the babies yours?"

The question caught him off guard. He wanted them to be. But they weren't. "Of course not," he muttered. "You know she had IUI with a sperm donor."

Janine shrugged. "I've seen doctors falsify charts for a friend. I'm not judging."

"Well, they're not mine," he growled. "You'll see that soon enough when you deliver them." Standing awkwardly, he carried Simone to the bed. "Do we need an ambulance?"

"What do you think?" Janine's grin was wry. He was acting like a total basket case.

"Sorry," he said. "She's stable. So, no."

"Go on, Hutch. Get yourself a stiff drink. I'll yell for you in a few minutes."

He paced from the bedroom down the hall to the kitchen. There he saw that Simone had tried to fix herself a sandwich. The jar of mustard was still open, and a grilled chicken breast languished on a plate.

The situation was unacceptable. He should have known from the beginning that she was going to need a babysitter. This kind of pregnancy was tricky. Simone was too inexperienced to know what she was facing.

It seemed like hours before Janine summoned him, but according to his watch, only twenty minutes had elapsed. He found Simone awake but chastened. Janine sat on the end of the bed. "I've given our patient a stern talking-to," she said.

"It's about time somebody did," he grumbled.

"I can't stay home for weeks and months," Simone wailed.

"Actually, you can." Janine's bark was worse than her bite, but the other doctor meant business. "Think about it, Simone. You're more fortunate than most. You own your own business. You have capable employees. Not only that, but you can keep tabs on things via your laptop. Now all we need is someone to play watchdog."

Hutch folded his arms across his chest. "That would be me," he said bluntly. At this point, he didn't care what Janine thought. Simone was still too damn pale. Her inky hair emphasized her pallor.

"No way," Simone said. She still had a bit of spunk left. "You have an important job."

"So I'll take some time off."

"You just got back from Africa," she cried. "You don't *have* any time off."

"Then I'll quit my job." His priorities were crystal clear. A sense of calm fatalism swept through him. He and Simone were bound by invisible threads. Maybe she didn't want him here, and maybe he shouldn't be here. But there it was. Some things defied explanation.

Janine watched both of them with speculation in her gaze. "Do you still want me to be her doctor?"

Hutch grimaced. "Of course." Then he looked at Simone. "Right?"

She glared at him. "Why ask now? It looks like you're prepared to take charge of my whole life."

Her sarcasm didn't faze him. "Damned straight."

Janine put her bag back together and checked Simone's pulse one more time. She smoothed a hand over Simone's flushed forehead. "Listen to the man. He may be arrogant, but he knows what he's doing. I'll feel a lot better knowing you're not living here on your own."

Simone's eyebrows shot to her hairline. "He can't move in here."

"Oh, yes, I can," Hutch said.

Janine grinned and stayed quiet.

The patient simmered. "What about gossip?" she said. Her gorgeous blue eyes were damp with tears.

Her vulnerability caught something in his chest and gave it a sharp squeeze. "I don't give a damn about gossip," he said. "What we do is our own business. My job is to take care of mothers and babies. For the foreseeable future, you're at the top of my list."

Janine nodded. "Sounds good to me. You have my number, Hutch. If you need me outside office hours, don't hesitate to call."

He kissed her cheek, overwhelmed with gratitude. "Thanks," he said gruffly.

Janine motioned toward the hall. Hutch followed

her, closing the door most of the way so they wouldn't be overheard. "Honestly, how is she doing?" he asked.

"I'm concerned that Simone is still losing weight, by her own admission. Even in cases of hyperemesis, we need to see her belly growing. She's as tiny as the first day I examined her. Force-feed her if you have to…little bits around the clock. But if those babies are going to have a chance, we need to strengthen their mother."

Hutch nodded. "When is her next ultrasound scheduled?"

"Not for another month. But under the circumstances, I think I'll bump it up. I want to make sure things are progressing."

"And if they're not?"

Janine shrugged. "You know the statistics. Don't alarm her more than necessary. But make her eat."

"You can count on it."

"I'll let myself out," Janine said. "Unless you want me to stay while you run home to pack a bag."

"It can wait until tomorrow. I'm sure one of her friends will come over if I call."

"I'm guessing she's been putting on a brave front."

He grimaced. "That would be Simone. Never let them see you sweat."

"Or in this case, barf."

Hutch chuckled. "Thank you for coming."

She cocked her head and stared at him. "Are you sure you know what you're doing?"

Janine had known him a long time. And she knew the history. "Not at all," he said. "But I don't really have a choice."

Nine

Simone overheard the last thing Hutch said to Dr. Fetter, and it cut her to the bone. *I don't really have a choice.* He was stuck with Simone because of some kind of moral obligation. Saint Hutch.

She bit her lip to keep from crying when he came back into the room. He still wore his white coat with Dr. Troy Hutchinson neatly embroidered on the chest. "Why are you doing this?" she asked wearily. "We can get Barb."

"Barb is overbooked as it is. Besides, I know you, Simone. You wouldn't be comfortable with a stranger in your house."

"*You're* practically a stranger," she shot back. "You've been gone for almost six years. Neither of us is the same person we used to be."

He didn't let her bait him. "That's a good thing, isn't it? Surely we've both grown up by now. I hope I have."

When Simone closed her eyes and didn't answer, he knew she was trying to shut him out. It didn't matter. Whatever the current relationship between them, he was going to protect her and her babies, God willing.

Shrugging out of his lab coat, he unbuttoned his blue dress shirt and rolled up the sleeves. The house was hot. Simone could use some fresh air. But the heat and humidity outside would only make her feel worse. He found the thermostat and made the AC click on. Soon, cool air began to blow out of the vents.

When he returned to the bedroom, Simone still had her eyes closed. He didn't know if she was resting or pouting. Grinning inwardly, he sat down on the edge of the bed and stroked her arm. "What if I fix scrambled eggs and bacon? That used to be your favorite." On the weekends in the old days, they would often spend most of their time in bed. When they were sated and content, they ended up in the kitchen eating breakfast for dinner.

Simone opened one eye. "With cinnamon toast?"

"Whatever you want, brave girl. All you have to do is ask."

Finally, he coaxed a smile from her. "That would be lovely," she whispered.

"And you'll stay in bed in the meantime?"

She nodded. "I will."

Fortunately, he found the kitchen stocked with basics. Soon, he had bacon sizzling as he worked on the toast. The eggs turned out fluffy and perfect. He hoped having the comfort food on hand would coax Simone into eating something, at least.

When he carried the tray to the bedroom, he realized that she had dozed off again. He wondered if she'd had trouble sleeping at night, or if it was her weakness making her drowsy. He set the tray on the bedside table and touched her arm. "Wake up, sleepyhead. Dinner is served." He guessed she had missed lunch entirely.

Simone struggled to sit up in bed. "That was fast."

Once she was settled, he sat down beside her. "I'm going to feed you," he said.

"I'm not a baby."

"No, but you're not a hundred percent. We'll take this slow. If we need to stop, we will."

She was visibly hesitant, but she eyed the plate longingly. "I want to gobble it up," she said glumly. "But that would be a disaster."

"I'm sure your stomach has shrunk. You won't be able to eat a normal meal yet. We'll get there gradually over the next few weeks. What do you want first?"

She wrinkled her nose. "Eggs, I think. I need the protein."

He offered her a forkful and nodded approvingly when she opened her mouth, chewed and swallowed. "So far, so good?"

Simone nodded. "You always were a better cook than me."

"Doesn't matter. You have other talents."

Her cheeks turned pink. She shot him a look from beneath her lashes, a look that made his blood run hot. "Naughty, naughty, Dr. Hutchinson. Are you trying to raise my blood pressure?"

"Whatever it takes, honey. Whatever it takes."

The gentle flirting reassured him. Simone looked a hell of a lot better now than when he'd first arrived and found her on the floor. He shuddered inwardly at the memory. If he had any say in the matter, she would never get to that point again.

His patient managed to eat half of the eggs, one piece of bacon and an entire slice of cinnamon toast. It was probably too much, but he didn't have the heart to refuse her when she was clearly starving.

She wiped her mouth with a napkin. "That was wonderful, Hutch. It seems to help when I don't have to be the one to fix it. Yesterday, I took one look at a raw egg and had to dash to the bathroom."

"Understandable. Let me clean up the kitchen, and then I have an idea."

The chore didn't take long, but once again, Simone was asleep when he returned. He decided to let her rest for a little bit. He needed to deal with a few urgent work situations if he was going to stay here semipermanently.

After half an hour of answering emails and texts, he was done, for the moment. Like Simone, part of his responsibilities could be dealt with remotely. His patient list was very small so far. Most of what he had been doing in these first few weeks was consulting on cases. Since he had access to the electronic records in his department, some things could go forward unchanged.

When he entered her bedroom this time, she was awake. Her color was better, and her eyes were brighter. "More dinner?" he asked.

"No. But so far, so good with what I ate."

"Excellent. I know you're exhausted, but what if we take one short stroll around the backyard? The exercise will do you good, and it will help you sleep more deeply. I'll be right beside you."

"Okay." She climbed out of bed on her own, waving him off when he tried to take her arm. "If this is going to work, you can't treat me like an invalid. I can go to the bathroom by myself."

He didn't like it, but he had to tread carefully with Simone. Her fierce independence was going to be at odds with his need to cosset her.

When they made it outdoors, the heat of the day had abated. The air was fresh and sweet. Simone's backyard was a rainbow of color, flowers blooming everywhere.

He put an arm around her waist. "Lean on me," he said. "And tell me if you need to stop."

They didn't speak as they made a lazy circuit of the premises. Simone's legs were shaky…that was easy to tell. But she powered on. By the time they made it back to the starting point, she was leaning on him heavily, and her breathing was rapid. He scooped her up in his arms and climbed the shallow steps.

"Good girl," he said softly. "I'm proud of you. Food and exercise. You'll make it yet."

"My hero," she smirked.

His lips twitching in amusement, he managed the knob and bumped the door open with his hip. "Do you want to go ahead and take a shower now? Or do you need to rest first?"

Simone looked up at him with big eyes. "Are you offering to join me, Doctor?"

"Do you need medical assistance?"

"I'm sure I do."

The little brat was taunting him, but there wasn't a chance in hell he was going to make love to her tonight. She knew the power she had over him, and she wasn't afraid to use it.

He deposited her on the bed and inspected the bathroom. If he put the tiny vanity stool in the shower, Simone wouldn't have to stand the whole time. "Okay," he said. "Let's do this."

She raised up on one elbow. "Don't you still keep a change of clothes in the car?"

Actually, he did, but he'd forgotten. Finding Simone semiconscious had thrown him off his game. "Why do you ask?"

"Well, if you're going to help me shower, you'll get soaked. You should go get what you need before we start."

"True."

She watched him intently.

"What are you thinking, Simone?" he asked. "I don't like that look."

"You know it makes sense for you to be naked, too."

Immediately and urgently, he was hard...painfully so. He schooled his expression not to reveal his physical turmoil. "I can take off my wet clothes when we're done. Stay put. I'll be back."

Outside, he put his hands on top of the car and banged his head softly against the metal door frame. He and Simone were playing a dangerous game of chicken, and he was losing. Grabbing the gym bag that held a clean pair of jeans, a knit shirt and underwear, he told himself he could be a gentleman.

Despite her propensity for suggestive repartee, Simone was in a fragile state. Even if she *wanted* to make love to him, she was in no condition to do so. He would help her with the shower and tuck her into bed. Period.

FREE Merchandise is 'in the Cards' for you!

Dear Reader,

We're giving away FREE MERCHANDISE!

Seriously, we'd like to reward you for reading this novel by giving you **FREE MERCHANDISE** worth over **$20** retail. And no purchase is necessary!

You see the Jack of Hearts sticker above? Paste that sticker in the box on the Free Merchandise Voucher inside. Return the Voucher today... and we'll send you Free Merchandise!

Thanks again for reading one of our novels—and enjoy your Free Merchandise with our compliments!

Pam Powers

Pam Powers

P.S. Look inside to see what Free Merchandise is **"in the cards"** for you!

W

e'd like to send you two free books like the one you are enjoying now. Your two books have a combined cover price of over $10 retail, but they are yours to keep absolutely FREE! We'll even send you 2 wonderful surprise gifts. You can't lose!

FREE MERCHANDISE VOUCHER

2 FREE BOOKS and **2 FREE GIFTS**

Please send my Free Merchandise, consisting of
2 Free Books and **2 Free Mystery Gifts**.
I understand that I am under no obligation to buy
anything, as explained on the back of this card.

225/326 HDL GLTD

Please Print

FIRST NAME

LAST NAME

ADDRESS

APT.#   CITY

STATE/PROV.   ZIP/POSTAL CODE

NO PURCHASE NECESSARY!

HD-517-FM17

READER SERVICE—Here's how it works:

Their first argument was over who would undress her. She stood at the bathroom counter, eyes blazing. "I can take off my own clothes, Hutch."

"If you get dizzy and fall, you'll hit something hard and smash your skull. You don't want that to happen, do you?"

"What I want is for you to treat me like an adult. Take off your own clothes, big boy." No man with an ounce of testosterone could resist such an all-out dare. He wasn't a teenager. He could control himself.

They stripped down side by side. Hutch tried not to look in the mirror. It was bad enough seeing Simone in the flesh. He didn't need to be surrounded with multiple images.

When he saw her completely naked for the first time, he cursed. The one and only time they had made love since he came home from Sudan, the room had been mostly dark. Now, in the bright light from the bathroom fixture, he took note of each feminine detail.

She crossed her arms over her breasts. "What's wrong?"

"I can see every one of your ribs, damn it. I can't believe how much weight you've lost."

"It's a new technique. I call it the triplet diet."

Even now, she was a smart-ass. "That's not funny." He couldn't decide if he wanted to spank her or kiss her.

Ignoring the urge to do either, he stepped past her to turn on the water and adjust the faucet. When he was satisfied the temperature was just right, he put the small stool in the large granite shower stall and took Simone's arm. "In you go."

She sat down with a small sigh. Closing her eyes,

she leaned her head against his hip. "Thank you, Hutch," she whispered. "For everything."

Tenderness came, overwhelming him and muting his physical need for her. "You're very welcome. Close your eyes and let me take care of you."

He started with shampoo, lathering Simone's long, dark tresses and rinsing with the handheld sprayer. Afterward, he grabbed the bottle of shower gel and soaped up a washcloth. Moving it over her shoulders and back, he made himself recite multiplication tables in his head to keep from going insane.

Her breasts were full and firm. When he soaped them lazily, the rosy nipples perked up. Eventually, he had washed everything he could reach. "Do you think you can stand for a minute?" he asked gruffly.

She nodded but didn't move.

"Do you want to do the rest yourself?"

Simone looked up at him with drowsy eyes. Her pupils were dilated; only a ring of deep azure remained. Her eyelashes were spiky and wet. "You're doing fine. Don't stop now." She put her hands on his forearms and drew herself upright.

Now her nose reached the center of his chest. He wanted to lift her and slide her down onto his rigid sex. He wanted to take her up against the wall of the shower and pound into her until the gnawing ache in his gut found release.

Instead, he did the honorable thing. He knelt and washed her feet and calves and thighs. Then, standing, with Simone embracing him, he rubbed between her legs.

Her breath caught audibly. "I want you," she whispered.

Hell. He shut his eyes and gritted his teeth. "We can't, sweet girl. Not today."

Their bodies were wet and slick and primed for action. But Simone was weak as a baby kitten. She fussed halfheartedly when he shut off the water and urged her out of the shower. As he dried her with a big fluffy towel, she murmured something he didn't quite catch. Afterward, he set her on the counter and grabbed another towel for himself.

Simone's back was to the mirror, her hair a tangled mess of black silk at her shoulders. "I'll have to dry your hair," he said. "It's too wet for you to get straight into bed."

He found a large-tooth comb and a hair dryer in one of the drawers. Simone seemed to be half asleep sitting up. Though he was clumsy at best, he managed to dry her hair until it was tangle-free.

She leaned into him. "You should do this for a living," she muttered, yawning.

"Only for you, kiddo." He picked her up and carried her to the bed. "Pajamas?"

Her smile was wicked. "Not tonight."

With shaking hands, he covered her all the way to the chin. "Go to sleep, Simone. I have some work to do, but I'll be in later. I'll take the other side of the bed."

"Will you be here when I wake up?" Her eyes had darkened, and for a moment, the impertinent facade slipped and he saw loneliness.

"I'm not going anywhere," he said firmly.

He pulled on the clean boxers and pants without the shirt. The house had cooled down some, but not enough. Or maybe he was the one who was overheated. Firing up his laptop and dealing with a backlog of email occupied him for an hour. Simone had an exercise bike in the guest room, so he did ten miles there. After that, he prowled, trying to convince himself he could lie in that bed with Simone and not go stark, raving mad.

During the course of the evening he had managed to get his erection under control for brief periods of time. Still, every moment he allowed his attention to wander, his libido took over, telling him how damn good it would feel to be intimate with Simone again.

His head was messed up, no doubt about it. First, there was the ghost of Bethany. The guilt he felt about her death might be illogical, but it lingered. Then there was Simone's unorthodox pregnancy. She was hiding something.

There were any number of men in Royal who would have been happy to provide sperm the old-fashioned way. What reason had been compelling enough to send Simone down this path?

He prayed unashamedly for her three babies. If she lost any or all of them, it would destroy him. Even more harrowing was the prospect of losing Simone. Women still died in childbirth occasionally. It was rare, but it happened. She wasn't his to lose, but he was the one in her court for the moment.

Finally, at eleven, he decided he was tired enough to go to sleep, no matter the provocation. He moved through the house checking locks and turning off the lights. By now, he knew his way around the master bedroom. He brushed his teeth with the toothbrush from last time. Leaning his hands on the counter, he gave himself a pep talk.

"Don't be stupid, Hutch. She doesn't need any

added stress, and you don't need the drama. She broke up with you the last time. Now she's in an even worse place to have a relationship with you. Get over it. Move on."

It was a good speech. Maybe even a great one. Despite that, when he stood beside the bed and studied the small lump under the covers, he rubbed his chest, trying to ease the ache there.

He'd always assumed he'd have a family one day, though not like this. Even if Simone had any residual feelings for him, he would have to wonder if she needed a father for her babies more than she needed a lover. It was a sobering thought.

Thankfully, he did sleep. And on his own side of the bed.

Once, toward dawn, he roused when Simone got up to go to the bathroom. He could see the outline of her nude body. "You okay?" he asked groggily.

"Yes."

She wasn't gone long. When she climbed back in bed, he could hear her breathing. "Hutch?" she said.

"Hmm?"

"Will you hold me?"

He inhaled sharply. "I don't think I can do that."

"Why not?"

Was she deliberately being obtuse, or did the woman truly not understand how badly he wanted her? "You're naked. I'm naked. Things will happen."

She chuckled. "Is that so terrible?"

Desperately, his better nature fought the good fight. "You're not one hundred percent."

"Then make love to what's left of me, please. And this time don't let go."

* * *

Simone knew she was being unfair. What was the penalty for tempting a saint? Eternal damnation? She had already tasted the depths of hell. When Hutch left for Sudan, she'd come close to falling apart completely. Only sheer force of will had enabled her to get out of bed and get dressed every day.

Eventually, the pain dulled. Work and friends and hobbies filled the hours. After a year, she dated again. Casually. Always, she wondered what would happen when Hutch came home. And then he didn't come home.

After the first three years, she had faced the bitter truth. By sending him off to fulfill his destiny, she had destroyed her chance at happiness with him. Even now, she was under no illusions. They had sexual attraction going for them, no question. But she was pregnant with another man's babies.

Lots of couples adopted children. This was different. Even if he could forgive her for the huge mistake she had made, surely he would want to father his own son or daughter.

What if she got pregnant again and it was as bad as this time? The thought of facing another nine months of misery was too wretched to contemplate. And four children? Simone didn't even know how to mother one or two or three, much less four.

The only thing left was hot sex with no strings attached. Even that would come to an end when she got embarrassingly huge.

With tears stinging her eyes, she met him in the middle of the mattress. "I'm not a very nice person," she whispered. "I should leave you alone."

He ran a hand down her flank, raising gooseflesh everywhere he touched. "I'm a big boy," he said. "I can handle it."

Ten

She reached for him in the dark, finding his erection and wrapping her hand around it. Hutch shuddered. She stroked him firmly, remembering instinctively what he liked. In the space of a hushed breath, the years melted away and the two of them were the same young, wildly infatuated couple they had once been.

Her body wasn't cooperating. She felt weak and barely able to move. Still, she wanted Hutch desperately. With the empathy that marked everything he did, he held her close and winnowed his fingers though her hair. "You're not up to this, Simone. Admit it."

His body was warm and hard and masculine against hers. The light fuzz of hair on his broad chest tickled her breasts and reminded her that he was a man in his prime. The stark contrast of tough male to soft female sent a shiver of delight down her spine. Having him wrap his muscular arms around her in a firm hug made her feel secure and cherished. He was right. She didn't have the energy for sex. Yet everything she knew told her to bind Hutch any way she could. She didn't want to lose him again. And she didn't want only his tender care. She wanted his love.

Dear God. The truth left her breathless. She still loved Troy Hutchinson. Illogically. Inescapably. Which meant she was destined for even greater heartbreak than before. The yawning hole in her chest was terrifying. She couldn't survive a second time. Especially not with babies in the mix.

As she lay there trembling, her change in mood must have alerted Hutch that something was wrong. He eased her onto her back and reclined on one elbow. Placing his hand, palm flat, on her stomach, he sighed. "Talk to me, honey. I'm not a mind reader."

"I shouldn't have gotten pregnant." She wanted to tell him the truth. She wanted to tell him why. But she was afraid he would look at her in disgust and disappointment.

"Your timing could have been better, that's true. But there's nothing wrong with wanting to become a mother."

Except that Simone had taken something so sacred and wonderful and used it for her own ends. "Are you still in love with Bethany?" She blurted it out, her pain and confusion erasing all sense of boundaries.

Hutch went still. He removed his hand. "Bethany has nothing to do with you and me," he said, the words flat.

"You didn't answer my question, Hutch." Why was she torturing herself? "Do you still love her?"

She heard him curse beneath his breath. His reaction was so out of character it shocked her.

"I will always love Bethany," he said. "She was selfless and pure in her devotion to the hurt and needy. She gave her life doing the things she considered essential for the good of humanity. She made me a better doctor…a better man. So, yes, Simone. I love Bethany. But she's gone, and I'm still here. If that's a problem, tell me now."

Her throat was so tight she could barely breathe, much less speak. Why had she wanted so badly to know the truth? Now she would never be able to forget what he'd said.

She touched his arm. "I'm sorry. You're right. She has nothing to do with us." Moving carefully, she climbed on top of him and buried her face in the curve of his neck. He was still hard and ready.

Hutch didn't need any further invitation. He lifted her hips and joined their bodies with a firm thrust. She cried out, the small sound muffled against his shoulder. He made love to her with such tenderness she wanted to weep. He was a doctor, yes. So he had taken an oath to do no harm. But this was more than that. He was coaxing her into trusting him, one heartbeat at a time.

What he couldn't know was that she would trust him with her life…and the lives of her babies. That wasn't the issue at all. The problem was the way she had let herself get twisted in knots over her grandfather's will and her feelings of not being able to measure up to her family's expectations.

It was too late now.

Hutch was hot, his taut body damp. He held her hips

in a grip that might bruise, though she didn't think he realized it. "Are you okay?" He ground out the words between clenched teeth.

She cupped his cheek with her hand, feeling the stubble on his face and chin. "I'm glad you came home, Hutch. I missed you." It wasn't an answer to his question. She wasn't okay…not at all. How could she tell him that she had been missing a part of herself for five long years?

At twenty-two, twenty-three, she hadn't understood how rare it was to find someone like Hutch. It shamed her to realize that if the situation arose now, she would beg him not to leave. In her youthful naïveté, she had assumed one of two things—either Hutch would come home after two and a half years and they would pick up where they left off, or she would eventually find someone else to love.

Neither scenario had been the case.

He rolled suddenly, taking her with him. She wrapped her legs around his waist and twined her arms around his neck. Hutch was wild now, his thrusts uncontrolled, his passion barely in check.

"Simone… Ah, hell…" He came with a groan that sounded more like pain than pleasure.

She wasn't even close. As much as she craved his touch, she was unable to summon the energy to climax. It was enough to know he wanted her.

In the aftermath, he moved them onto their sides and held her gently, stroking her hair and feathering kisses over her eyelids and cheekbones.

"I remembered this," he said quietly. "In Sudan. When things got bad. Sometimes we lost babies who should have lived. Mothers, too. It ate me up inside.

When I couldn't sleep at night, I would imagine you in bed with me. It helped. It anchored me."

"But you didn't come home the first time." She heard the note of accusation in her own voice. "That sounded angry," she added quickly. "And I wasn't. I'm not." What she had been was devastated.

He sighed, his breath stirring the hair at her temple. "I was going to," he said. "I had every intention of coming back to Royal when my first tour was over. But…"

"But what?"

"You and I had ended things on a difficult note. I wasn't sure there was any reason to come home. And the need in West Darfur was overwhelming. You were so damn young when we broke up. It occurred to me that I was probably someone to experiment with… someone unsuitable you could toss in your parents' faces to prove you were a grown woman."

Simone flinched, incredibly hurt. "It wasn't that. It was never that, Hutch. I adored you."

"But not enough to beg me to stay."

"That's not fair."

"I knew you were ambitious. I knew you wanted to be successful. You had life in the palm of your hand. It's not surprising that my life and yours didn't mesh."

"I was trying to do the right thing," she said bitterly. "For once in my life, I was being unselfish." *And look where it got me…*

He sighed. "Why don't we agree to let the past stay in the past? Neither of us handled the relationship well."

"And now?"

"What do you mean?" His question held a tinge of wariness.

"Are we handling *this* well?"

"How the hell should I know? I'm an obstetrician, not a shrink."

Simone was shocked when he rolled away from her and left the bed. "Where are you going? It's still dark out."

"I need to clear my head," he said gruffly. "Go back to sleep."

Hutch didn't wait to see if she obeyed his command. Her scent was on his skin. The sound of her voice echoed in his head. His heart pounded as adrenaline surged through his veins. He either wanted to run or to fight or to climb back into his lover's bed and stake a claim.

It was easy to pretend that Simone was the same woman he'd left behind. Easy, for now. When her pregnancy began to show, all bets were off. Every time he looked at her, he would be reminded that she had made a choice to be a single mom. It still made no sense. Simone was the quintessential career woman. Not only that, she was far too young to worry about her biological clock.

He let himself out of the house quietly and prowled the backyard. At this hour, the air was cool and sweet. Janine Fetter was no gossip, but sooner or later, word would filter around town. Simone Parker was pregnant. And Troy Hutchinson was living in her house.

Did he care? That was the million-dollar question. People would make assumptions about Simone's pregnancy. It was only natural. Undoubtedly, some folks around Royal would believe he had returned from Africa so that he and Simone could pick up where they left off.

If anybody did the math, they would know he wasn't the father of her triplets. But was anybody going to be following their situation that closely?

For one brief moment, he considered offering Simone a version of what they'd had in the past. Not his heart. That wasn't up for grabs. Something else instead. She was going to need help. He liked having regular sex with someone he cared about.

There were worse reasons to hook up.

Still, there was no rush. He was here to make sure she took care of herself. In the meantime, he could decide if they were actually compatible. Simone liked to jump in the deep end without pondering the consequences. He was a planner, a cautious man who preferred to calculate the risks.

Maybe it would work. Maybe it wouldn't. He had time to decide.

After that first night, their time together fell into a routine of sorts. The mornings were hardest for Simone. He was a decent cook, so he tempted her with light fare, anything he thought she would enjoy and be able to keep down.

Gradually, her color improved and she became stronger—strong enough to want to go back to work.

They argued ten times a day, it seemed. Him pointing out that she had a long way to go in this pregnancy, Simone insisting he was a worrywart. In the end, they compromised.

He'd been sleeping under her roof for seven nights

when Simone revealed the real reason she was desperate to get back to work. While Hutch made grilled cheese sandwiches and tomato soup for both of them, Simone sat at the kitchen counter with her laptop and fretted.

"I'm in charge of this upcoming charity event," she said, waving her hands. "It was my idea. I can't let the preparations slide anymore or we'll never be ready."

He listened with half an ear, wondering if the rough weather that buffeted the windows would turn into a tornado watch. He'd been in Sudan when a killer storm leveled big chunks of Royal a few years ago. People were still antsy whenever the skies turned dark.

Simone tossed a paper wad at him. "Pay attention, Hutch. I'm trying to explain."

He shrugged with an unrepentant grin. Now that Simone was feeling slightly better, she talked his ear off. "I'm sorry," he said. "Go ahead. I'm listening. What's it called again?"

"Nothing yet," she grumbled. "That's part of the problem. The invitations need to go out by Monday, and I have everything ready but the name."

Royal's hardworking charity organization, Homes and Hearts, was slated to be the beneficiary of Simone's latest PR idea. When she fell ill recently, she'd been in the midst of planning a grand masquerade ball to raise money to build more houses for the homeless.

Instead of hosting at the Cattleman's Club, Simone and Cecelia had cooked up the idea of christening the grand ballroom at Deacon Chase's new five-star resort, The Bellamy. He and Shane Delgado had been inspired by the Biltmore House in Asheville, North Carolina, though their architectural baby here in Royal was hip-per and more modern. Sitting amid fifty-plus acres of lush gardens, The Bellamy was lavish and expensive.

Simone had declared it the perfect location.

"How about Masks for Mortar?" he said. "Has a ring to it, don't you think?"

Simone squealed and jumped off the stool, rounding the island to hug him enthusiastically. "That's perfect, Hutch. Let me insert that line in the file, and I'll get it off to the printer."

"Don't you need somebody else's approval? I don't want to be responsible if the idea bombs." He was only half kidding.

"It's exactly right," she insisted.

While she futzed with her email, he shoved a plate under her nose. "Here's your lunch, Simone."

She nodded absently. "Put it right there. I'll try a few bites."

Leaning over the counter, he closed her laptop. "Eat now. Doctor's orders."

He wasn't going to budge on this one. It pleased him to see her so happy, but she could easily get into trouble again if she didn't make sure to nibble when her stomach was actually cooperating.

She made a face at him. "Dictator."

"Shrew." He grinned. Gradually, they were becoming less cautious with each other. It was a good sign, but he was pretty sure the détente was only temporary.

For one thing, Simone never talked about the babies. She let Hutch check her blood pressure twice a day, and she ate as much as she was able to. Other than that, there was no outward indication that anything was going on beneath the surface.

One afternoon a week or so later, she seemed moodier than usual.

He tugged the end of her ponytail. "What's bugging you?"

"I'm almost three months along. When will I feel them move?"

Suddenly, he realized she was still fretting about the pregnancy. "Well…" He hesitated, trying to speak the truth without offering false promises. "Every day that passes brings you one day closer to a successful outcome. In a normal pregnancy, you'd likely start to notice the baby moving at five months."

"But with triplets?"

"Could be sooner. Could be later."

"And for that sound medical judgment you went to med school…"

Her snarkiness amused him. "Things are going well," he said gently.

Simone bit her bottom lip. "Dr. Fetter wants me to come in for the ultrasound tomorrow."

"I know."

"What if…"

He put his hand over her mouth and kissed her nose. "The ultrasound will make you feel better."

"Or maybe not," she mumbled against his fingers.

"Are we having the glass half-empty, half-full conversation?"

Her blue eyes glistened with tears. Like bluebonnets in the rain. He knew he was in trouble when he realized he was waxing poetic, even in his head.

Simone wriggled until he released her. She wrapped her arms around her waist. "You don't understand. As long as I'm standing here with you in this kitchen, those three babies are alive and developing normally. I don't want to go to the hospital and find out differently."

He wondered if any of the other people in her life knew that beneath Simone's facade of bravado and confidence lurked a sensitive, vulnerable woman. "I'll go with you," he said. "It will be fine. And if it's not, you can lean on me."

"I have to do this alone," she insisted, her chin set in stubborn mode.

"No, you don't. That's ridiculous."

"I'm serious, Hutch. It's one thing for you to stay here and make sure I eat. It's a whole other ball game for you to parade up to that hospital with me when everybody in the building knows who you are. I can't deal with that, too. You can drive me there if you insist, but I want you to drop me off at the door and leave."

His temper started to boil. "You're being absurd."

"Don't patronize me," she snapped. The tears spilled over now. "Leave me alone," she cried. "I'm going to my room."

He told himself pregnant women were at the mercy of roller-coaster hormones. Simone needed her space.

It made sense. The artificial situation in which they found themselves was beginning to fray at the seams. After the first night of his stay, he hadn't made love to her at all. He'd wanted to, God knew, but he had felt the need to back up and reassess. He'd been sleeping in the guest room ever since. Alone.

If Simone really cared about him as more than a doctor and a friend, she would make the first move. But she hadn't.

A crack of thunder right over the house made him

jump. He was horny and frustrated and angry at himself for getting involved with a woman who had far too many issues at play.

The fact that she didn't want him in the room when she had the ultrasound done was a red flag. He wanted to protect her and keep her from any kind of pain, physical or mental.

What Simone wanted was a mystery.

Her sandwich and soup sat uneaten on the counter. He zapped the plate in the microwave and carried it down the hall as a peace offering.

He found the bedroom door ajar. Simone sat in the middle of the carpet with a strange look on her face. He set the tray on the dresser and squatted beside her. "Is this some new yoga pose I don't know about?" he asked lightly.

She raised the hem of her shirt, took his hand and placed it flat on her belly. "I have a baby bump, Hutch. I really do!"

Eleven

She actually did. Only someone who had studied her body as much as he had would have been able to tell, but it was legit. He stroked her stomach. "You do, indeed. A real baby bump. Congratulations."

Simone rested her head against his knee. "I know it sounds stupid, but I was afraid nothing was there."

"And you were deathly ill because…" He raised an eyebrow.

"I said it didn't make sense."

Being so close to her after a week of strained celibacy filled his body with a fine tension. He rose to his feet. "You still haven't eaten lunch. I hate to beat a dead horse, but I'm not willing to see you back in the shape you were in before." He reached out a hand to help her to her feet.

"I'll eat, I swear. But Hutch…" She looked up at him, her eyes sparkling.

"What?"

"I'm feeling lots better."

The look on her face spelled trouble for him. Especially because he hadn't decided what he wanted from her or what Simone needed from him. "I'm glad," he said, pretending to misunderstand her artless invitation.

"Are you going to make me beg?" She wrapped her arms around his waist and rested her cheek right over his heart—or what was left of it.

He'd spent hours wondering why this woman still had the power to move him. It was more than the past they shared, though that was part of it. It was also more than the fact that he felt protective of her as a mother-to-be in the midst of a high-risk pregnancy.

Even now, he was afraid to name the emotion that made him hold her close. He wouldn't cheapen it by calling it lust. But he couldn't say it was love. He'd loved two women in his life, and both relationships had ended badly. Maybe he was using Simone. Maybe she was using him. In the end, what did it matter? They were emotionally and physically entangled, for better or for worse.

"I assume you're talking about sex?"

She leaned back and scowled at him. "Don't be so stuffy, Doctor."

"You still haven't eaten your lunch." Though he tried to stave off the inevitable, he was hard and ready. And he was pretty sure Simone knew it.

"Bring me the damned sandwich," she said.

"And the soup."

"Oh. My. Gosh. You're going to drive me insane."

He scooped her up in his arms and dumped her on

the bed. "I'd say that's a two-way street." He liked carrying her. Some people thought doctors had a God complex. Hutch didn't. At least, he didn't think so. However, he *would* cop to being an inveterate caretaker. It was in his blood.

When he grabbed the food and turned back around, he stumbled. Simone had stripped off her top and bra and was starting in on the rest of her clothes. "You said you would eat," he pointed out. It was hard to speak because his throat was so dry.

She crooked a finger. "I didn't say when."

Even a highly trained medical professional had his limits. He abandoned the meal tray so quickly it was a wonder he didn't spill tomato soup all over Simone's beautiful carpet. "Damn it, woman. Move over."

Simone was giddy. For the first time in days she felt almost like herself. Even more important, she saw tangible proof of her pregnancy. The change in her belly was infinitesimal, but it was real. Without Hutch's careful attention, she might have become so ill that she miscarried. Instead, he had watched over her day and night, despite the fact that she was pregnant under the worst of circumstances.

Her heart overflowed. Everything that had drawn her to him six years ago was still there: his patience, his sense of humor, his deep commitment to his calling. In some ways, *she* was the one who was different. And in the midst of that fresh perspective, she found herself falling more deeply in love with him than ever before.

In the years Hutch had been gone, Simone had grown and matured. Even in her misguided attempt to become a mother, she had found new meaning in her life. The babies she carried were a sacred responsibility.

If she could have her way, she would kneel beside the bed and propose to Hutch. *Marry me. Make a family with me.* But that would be so unfair. So she did the next best thing. She gave herself to him and demanded nothing in return.

She hadn't truly understood what it cost him to stay out of her bed the past few days. Not until now. He was flushed and desperate, his body pinning hers to the bed as his teeth raked the curve of her neck. His intensity didn't frighten her. She understood it in the marrow of her bones.

No force on earth could have kept them apart.

He handled her roughly, with little foreplay. They kissed wildly. She wrestled with him and taunted him, for nothing more than the pleasure of being subdued. He manacled her wrists in one big hand and tried to mount her. She eluded him but didn't get far. They rolled from one side of the mattress to the other, kicking the sheets aside in their frenzy. Hutch muttered her name along with a few choice expletives.

Laughing out loud, she bit his earlobe. "I love you this way," she whispered. "Take what you want. Make me submit. Do it, Hutch."

When he moved between her thighs and thrust all the way in with one deep push, she cried out. "Don't stop. Don't stop."

He took her at her word. She had waved a red flag in front of the bull, and now he was crazed. He rode her hard. Never had she seen him so greedy, so dangerously male. Maybe she had wanted to make him snap. Maybe she reveled in his physical need for her.

Even so, his total absorption was shocking. And thrilling.

Her climax hit hard. Hutch groaned, his face buried in her hair. She clenched him with her inner muscles, wresting from each of them the last ripples of pleasurable sensation. Then he shuddered, his body went rigid and he slumped on top of her.

Time ceased to have meaning. The Grecian shades at her bedroom windows were open, letting the harsh midday sun flood the room. Hutch might have been asleep. She wasn't sure. She didn't know whether to let out an exultant sigh or to burst into tears.

When he didn't move, she surmised that he really was out cold. It was no wonder. He'd spent the last week wandering the halls at night, making sure she was okay. The man had to be exhausted.

Silently, she eased out from under him and went to the bathroom to clean up. Afterward, she put her clothes back on and examined the cold sandwich and soup. The simple meal was a truce flag of sorts. Wrinkling her nose, she made herself eat three-fourths of it.

Perhaps it would have made more sense to go back to the kitchen and heat it up, but she wanted to be around when Hutch roused. She wasn't about to climb back into bed to eat. Though there were two chairs in the bedroom, she didn't like the idea of balancing the tray on her lap. In the end, she sat on the floor, legs crossed, and leaned back against the dresser.

He opened his eyes without drama. One minute he was dead to the world—the next he was completely alert.

"Did you eat?" he asked.

She shook her head at his single-mindedness and

held out her hand, indicating what little was left of the meal. "As promised."

Hutch nodded. "Good." Without fanfare, he climbed out of bed, picked up his clothes and disappeared into the bathroom.

She was rapidly discovering that sex in the daytime was far different than sex at night. There was literally nowhere to hide. Not that Hutch had any apparent qualms about his nudity. Fortunately, she was completely clothed.

The urge to escape was humiliating, but she gave in to it, anyway. It was *her* house, her bedroom. Why did she feel the need to disappear?

In the kitchen, she rinsed her lunch dishes and put them in the dishwasher. Hutch still hadn't made an appearance. Chewing her lip, she sat down in front of her laptop. Remembering how he had shut it without her permission should have made her angry. Instead, it made her sad.

Deep in her heart she wanted Hutch to be her date at the masquerade ball. Assuming, of course, she was well enough to attend when the time came. Unfortunately, she sensed that the two of them were fast approaching a showdown. They couldn't go on as they were.

After giving the mock-up of the invitation one last edit, she hit Send. The card stock and envelopes had been selected days ago. The printer already had a list of the recipients and would take care of the mailing. After that, it was only a matter of how many invitees would RSVP with a yes.

Cecelia and Naomi were supposed to drop by tomorrow afternoon to finalize decorating plans, not only for the tables, but for the ballroom as a whole. Deacon had given them carte blanche to spend whatever necessary to make this a night Royal would never forget.

With that one pressing chore completed, Simone pulled up the Neiman Marcus website. She visited the flagship store in Dallas a couple of times a year, but hadn't been recently. Fortunately, even though she had been too sick to travel, her personal shopper several hundred miles away had dropped images of four exclusive ball gowns into Simone's shopping cart.

She clicked on them one at a time. Buying this kind of dress while pregnant might ordinarily have been a risky roll of the dice. But she had lost so much weight, she knew she would still be able to get into her regular size.

With the prospect of a late-stage pregnancy in her future, it seemed only natural to want to look her best on the special night that was rapidly approaching. Two of the dresses were black, another white and the last one was a vibrant red. Although the guests would be asked to wear masks, the evening was formal. No Tin Man and Dorothy or Darth Vader costumes for this crowd.

Royal's elite would be out in full force wearing tuxedos and couture fashion. Both of the black dresses on her computer screen were beautiful and undeniably suitable for the occasion. But she didn't feel a strong connection to either one. The white dress was sexy, but a little too bridal for an unwed mother-to-be.

That left only the red. With Simone's jet-black hair, the vivid color would be dramatic in the extreme, and the style of the dress was perfect. The halter neckline would leave her shoulders bare. The back would plunge to the base of her spine. Though there were no adornments at all, the fabric was a slubbed-silk blend that would hopefully move and sway as she walked.

Only by trying them on could she decide for sure. She selected the red dress and added one of the black ones in case her first choice didn't work. With overnight express shipping, she would still have plenty of time to shop for other options if neither of these fit well.

She was reaching for her credit card in her purse when Hutch startled her.

"Retail therapy?" he asked casually, dropping a kiss on top of her head.

"How do you do that?" she said.

"Do what?"

"Walk like a ghost."

He shrugged. "Lots of night rounds. We learned not to wake the patients unless absolutely necessary."

"Ah."

He sat at the opposite side of the counter and stared at her. "We need to talk."

She nodded glumly. "I know."

"I would like to go with you to the ultrasound tomorrow."

That wasn't what Simone had expected him to say. She shook her head. "I've already explained why that's not a good idea."

"And I've already told you I want to be there."

"Please don't make this difficult."

His gaze narrowed. "You're the one who's throwing up barriers. Are you saying it's okay for us to sleep together but not to be seen in public?"

"Not at the hospital," she muttered. She was still holding out hope that Hutch would be her date for the masquerade ball, although to be fair, they would all be wearing masks, so even then no one had to know Hutch and Simone were a couple. Sort of… Who was she kidding? The man had a serious presence and would be recognized—mask or no mask.

Usually in the wake of sexual satisfaction, men were relaxed and mellow. Hutch was livid. His jaw was carved from stone, and his brown eyes burned. "Okay then." He reached for his own laptop, unplugged it and tucked it into the sleek leather briefcase monogrammed with his initials.

Simone frowned. "What are you doing?"

"I'm leaving." He never even looked at her as he calmly gathered his pens and billfold and hospital ID.

Panic made her stomach cramp. "Why?"

"Don't be naive, Simone."

"Tell me," she said, distraught. "The ultrasound is no big deal."

"I'm a doctor," he said, the words colder than any she had ever heard him utter. "Of course it's a big deal. But this is about more than ultrasounds, isn't it? You're making sure that no one but Janine knows we have any kind of connection. I was prepared to be a friend to you and these babies, but you don't need any more friends, do you, Simone?"

She grabbed his arm as he started to walk out of the room. "I don't want you to go," she said. Her heart cracked along fault lines years in the making.

He shrugged her off. "You're eating a suitable amount now. The nausea has subsided to manageable levels. There is absolutely no reason for me to remain. Or am I wrong?"

His gaze was impassive. Yet beneath his icy calm, she understood that he was daring her to do something. Anything.

The trouble was, she had no clue how he felt about her. Could she bear to have a relationship with him knowing the sainted Bethany would always be a ghost in their bed? And even if she could make peace with being second best, would Hutch ever want to be more than her friend? Was he interested in any kind of permanent role as stepparent?

Why would he be? He had the world at his feet.

During a split second when time stood still, mocking her indecision, she imagined and discarded half a dozen scenarios for her future. In none of them was there any real possibility that Hutch would be included.

So she tamped down her terror and her desperation and lifted her chin. "No," she said quietly. "No reason at all."

She had honestly thought she couldn't sink any lower than the miserable days of severe nausea and collapse. But it turned out she was wrong. Watching a stern-faced Troy Hutchinson walk out of her house without a backward glance sent a knife through her chest.

The pain was so intense, she thought she might pass out. She clung to the counter, her breathing shallow and rapid, and tried to stop shaking. Life was so unfair. Why had Troy come back to her at such an inauspicious moment? Why did she still love him when he had left his heart in Africa?

Why had she ever thought her grandfather's will was such a big deal?

In the space of a few weeks, all of her priorities had changed. It was a sobering realization to understand that every single one of her heartaches and heartbreaks was of her own creation.

She wasn't able to sleep in her bed that night. Instead, she went to the guest room and curled up in a ball where Troy had lain. The sheets still smelled like him. She cried for an hour and then made herself stop. It was no longer possible to be the same self-centered, ego-driven woman she had once been.

By this time next year, she would have three infants living under her roof. Hutch or no Hutch, that was her reality. It would have been easy to blame the babies for her situation. Without them, perhaps she and Hutch might have found their way back together for good.

Even reeling from the afternoon's trauma, she had to face the truth. Hutch was gone. The babies were here to stay. And she was their mama. Bless their hearts. Already, she knew they deserved better.

Somehow, she would pick herself up and go on. Somehow…but not tonight. Tonight, she would grieve, and if she was lucky, perhaps she wouldn't dream about the good doctor at all.

Twelve

When morning came, she tried to avoid looking in the mirror. She knew she was haggard and pale. At least she was strong enough to drive. Her stomach was a little queasy, but that had more to do with heartbreak and a sleepless night than her pregnancy.

She showered and styled her hair on autopilot. Choosing something to wear, once a pivotal point in her daily routine as a young twentysomething, now barely merited a moment's thought. The only reason she cared at all was that she didn't want anyone to feel sorry for her.

With that in mind, she chose a sunshine-yellow dress, sleeveless with white trim, and paired it with cork-heeled sandals. Normally, she used foundation only for special occasions. She'd been blessed with good skin.

Today, though, she needed help covering up the deep shadows beneath her dull eyes. Mascara and brightly colored lip gloss gave her a semblance of health, but if anyone looked closely enough, they wouldn't be fooled.

Frankly, she was terrified. She knew the ultrasound itself was painless, but what the test would reveal was a mystery. If she had asked either Naomi or Cecelia, both would have volunteered to come with her. Was it pride or a need to lick her wounds that kept her from contacting her two best friends?

She would see them later today. If the news she received at the hospital was bad, she wouldn't be able to hide her grief. Maybe that was for the best. They were the only people who would be able to help, the only ones who knew her inside and out.

Much like before, the ultrasound tech was professional but frustratingly uncommunicative when it came to explaining the images on the screen. Simone lay on the table with her eyes closed and prayed.

At last it was over. She dressed again in her cheerful outfit and managed a smile when the tech escorted her to an exam room. Then came the usual pokes and prods. Her blood pressure was a tad low. The scale showed she had lost ten pounds since her last visit. The nurse's expression of consternation was quickly masked, but Simone knew she should be gaining.

The last hurdle was waiting for Dr. Fetter. There was no need for a pelvic exam today. The only reason Simone had come to the hospital was to discuss the ultrasound. So she clasped her hands in her lap and waited.

Twenty-seven-and-a-half minutes. Could have been

worse. Janine Fetter burst through the door with a quick apology. "I've got two babies in progress, one about to deliver three weeks early. But we have a few hours yet. Let's take a look at these pictures so you can be on your way."

The other woman opened Simone's record on the laptop. The tech had already uploaded the images. The doctor studied them for interminable minutes, flipping from screen to screen, and finally looked up with a smile. "Congratulations, Simone. As far as I can tell, you have three extremely healthy fetuses. Barring any unforeseen circumstances, I think we're past the immediate danger point."

"But what about all the weight I've lost?" Simone asked, afraid to give in to relief too fast.

Dr. Fetter stood up and tucked her reading glasses in the pocket of her lab coat. "That's the wonderful thing about babies. They've been taking all the nutrition they need. You're the one who's fragile right now, not them. Since your nausea is easing to a great degree, I'm confident we'll see your weight bounce back in the coming weeks."

"Oh…"

The doctor cocked her head. "Simone?"

"Yes, ma'am?"

"You can drop the *ma'am*. I'm not that old."

"Sorry."

"My job is to take care of you and your babies, not to pry into your personal business. But…" She trailed off with a wince.

"But what? Go ahead. Say what you're thinking."

"I don't think you understand what you're facing."

The doctor's lack of faith hurt. "I'm doing my best," Simone said stiffly.

"It's not that. I'm talking about *after* the pregnancy. Having triplets is not a solo event. It requires coordinated teamwork. For quite some time."

"Naomi and Cecelia have promised to help me."

"That's lovely, and I'm sure they mean well, but neither of them knows babies, do they?"

"No. Isn't it a kind of learn-as-you-go thing?"

"Yes and no. Giving birth to triplets means having your life scheduled beyond belief. It means *at least* three adults holding, feeding and diapering three babies around the clock until they begin sleeping through the night. Are your parents physically capable of helping you?"

Simone shook her head. "Physically, maybe, but not emotionally. They won't be the warm, fuzzy kind of grandparents."

"Pardon me for asking, but what about Dr. Hutchinson?"

Simone froze inside. "What about him?"

The doctor clearly tried to choose her words with care. "If there is something between you—if he is willing to help—I think it would be in your best interests to let him."

"And that doesn't strike you as a poor bargain for Hutch?"

"Troy Hutchinson is a grown man. I'm sure he can make those decisions for himself."

Simone left the hospital in a daze. She was thrilled her pregnancy was not in danger. Even so, the confirmation that she would be giving birth to three babies was shockingly real.

She returned home just as Naomi and Cecelia pulled into her circular driveway. Hugging them both, she blinked away stupid tears. "Thanks for coming. I really want to finish all the details for the masquerade ball. The nausea is better for the moment, but it might come back again. I want all my ducks in a row before that happens."

"*If* it happens," Naomi insisted as she gathered up a stack of file folders and followed the other two up the steps.

Cecelia nodded. "Think positive."

Simone didn't shoot back with a sarcastic retort. Naomi was entitled to her optimism. After all, she was the only one not slated to be a parent in the near future. Cecelia, on the other hand, should know better. Even though she seemed to be sailing through her own pregnancy, surely she didn't think the rigors of childbirth and motherhood could be withstood using perky catchphrases.

Suddenly, the truth dawned on Simone. Cecelia wouldn't be any help at all with the triplets. She and Deacon would have their own bundle of joy. How had Simone ignored that glaring reality? Maybe because Cecelia seemed so normal. Not to mention the fact that the three friends had barely seen each other in the past few weeks.

As the other two women spread all their work on the dining room table, Simone grabbed a handful of plain crackers. "You want anything?" she asked.

Naomi shook her head. "I'm good."

Cecelia declined, as well. "Let's get started," she said. "We have a lot to do."

Planning an event of this magnitude was fun but challenging. Cecelia had struggled at length with color-coded spreadsheets to work out the placement of tables in the large room. The final information would be transferred onto diagrams so the volunteers and hotel staff would have something to work from during decorating and setting the tables.

Naomi, a gifted amateur artist, had sketched out three different themes and color palettes for the event as a whole. "I like the silver and navy," she said. "But do we need an accent color?"

Simone and Cecelia studied the other two contenders. Cecelia pointed at the brightest of the lot. "These colors are great, but they remind me more of a beachy summer event."

"I agree," Simone said. "And I think the burgundy and gray is *too* dark."

Naomi nodded. "So we're going with the silver and navy?"

Cecelia nodded. "I do like it the best. We could always add some pops of crimson."

"Perfect," Naomi said.

Simone jotted notes in her phone. Pregnancy brain must be a real condition, because she was already having trouble remembering things. She hoped one of the dresses she had ordered would fit. With the color scheme they had selected, the red would work nicely.

After an hour, most of the urgent decisions had been made. Naomi yawned, still in the midst of jet lag. Cecelia excused herself to call Deacon about something. Simone nibbled the end of her fingernail.

"Naomi," she said quietly.

"Hmm…" Her friend blinked and sat up straight. "Sorry. I should have flown home yesterday. Early-morning flights are a killer."

"Do you still think me getting pregnant is a terrible idea?"

Naomi lifted an eyebrow. "Does it matter? That horse is out of the barn, if you'll pardon the expression."

"Well, duh. But yes, it does matter."

"Why?"

Simone jumped to her feet and took a glass out of the cabinet, keeping her back to Naomi so the other woman couldn't see her face. "I know you won't lie to me."

"Damn." Naomi sighed. "Nothing like being boxed into a corner. Look at me when I say this."

"That bad, is it?" Simone managed a smile.

Naomi drummed her fingers on the countertop. "I don't understand why you did it. I don't know how in the world you're going to manage. I'm worried about the risks of childbirth and a complicated pregnancy. I'm feeling like an outsider while you and Cecelia are in some special club I can't understand. I'm confused about why Troy Hutchinson is hanging around. I know I want to help you, but my on-camera schedule is not very flexible right now. The whole situation seems like a recipe for disaster."

"Wow…" A tear rolled down Simone's cheek.

"Let me finish." Naomi stood up and wrapped her arms around Simone. "I know you, Simone. I know your generous heart and your loyalty. I've seen you make big mistakes, but I've always noted how hard you work to overcome them. If you want babies, then by damn, I'm going to play the auntie role to the hilt. And if anybody in Royal has the guts to criticize you, they'll have to answer to me."

Simone sniffed. "I think I got snot on your shirt."

"No worries."

"It's a designer piece, isn't it?"

Naomi gave her one last hug and released her. "Gucci. But my dry cleaner is a miracle worker."

Cecelia returned right about then, all starry-eyed from her conversation with her fiancé. She stared at the two in the kitchen. "What did I miss?"

"Not a thing," Naomi said. "Simone was being stupid, but I straightened her out."

Cecelia sniffed. "You shouldn't be unkind to a pregnant woman. We need to be cossetted."

Simone shook her head ruefully. Cecelia—blonde, tall and gorgeous on any given day—was absolutely radiant right now. "I'm fine. Believe me."

Naomi changed the subject. "Have either of you heard any more about the mysterious Maverick?"

Simone felt her face freeze. She knew she should disclose the contents of her own threatening email, but she was afraid. "The rumor in town is that he or she has gone underground. Things have been suspiciously quiet."

Cecelia huffed. "Good riddance, I say. After the pain he caused me and some of the other members of the TCC, he should be prepared for backlash."

After that, the conversation drifted back to the upcoming masquerade ball. Simone ordered pizza for the three of them. When it arrived, they all sat in the backyard to enjoy the evening.

By eight o'clock Simone was drooping. "I hate to run you off, but I have an old-lady bedtime right now." The fatigue came in waves, threatening to squash her beneath its weight.

They walked back through the house and out onto the front porch. After exchanging hugs, Naomi slid behind the wheel of her car. She had picked up Cecelia on the way. "Call us if you need anything."

Cecelia nodded. "I don't like you being here alone. What happened to the yummy Dr. Hutchinson?"

"He has a job, you know." Simone managed a cheery smile. "I'm doing lots better. Don't worry about me."

As the car drove away, she bit her lip, hard enough to remind herself that she was a proud, strong, independent woman. She didn't need Naomi or Cecelia or even Hutch to hold her hand for the next six months.

After turning off the lights and locking up the house, she took a shower and curled up in her bed with the TV remote. She was too restless to read.

Hutch was gone. She might as well get used to it.

The trouble was, everywhere she looked, she saw him. Laughing at her in the kitchen…caring for her in the bedroom when she was too sick to stand…holding her up as he coaxed her through laps around the backyard.

The man was a healer. Looking after the needy was what made him tick. She couldn't and shouldn't read too much into the fact that he had made himself available as her round-the-clock personal physician.

Really personal. She moved restlessly in the bed. It was humiliating to realize that despite his disdain and their argument and his icy exit, she still wanted him.

Glancing at the clock, she saw that it was only nine

forty-five. Earlier, she'd been exhausted. Now, with yearning and arousal pulsing through her veins, she had no desire to sleep. At all. With a mutter of ridicule for her own foolishness, she climbed out of bed. After putting on old jeans and a soft cotton sweater in blue and gray stripes, she shoved her feet into espadrilles and tossed her hair up in a ponytail.

She didn't have a clue about the location of Hutch's temporary apartment. But she did know which house he had bought. It was the only one for sale in her neighborhood. Suddenly, her curiosity overcame her good sense.

The pizza she had eaten earlier rolled suspiciously in her stomach, but she ignored it. She was on an investigative mission. Soon, Hutch was going to be living very close to her. What if he brought beautiful women home with him? What if Simone saw them arriving and departing in a steady stream? How was she going to handle that?

The For Sale sign was still up in the front yard, but the Realtor had tacked a Sold banner diagonally across the original notice. Simone parked in the driveway and got out. The landscaping looked scruffy. Nothing a master gardener couldn't take care of in a week or two.

Unlike Simone's more modern home, this was one of the last original structures on the street. It probably dated back to the earliest days of Royal. She remembered that the previous owner, or maybe the one before him, had gutted the inside and created a more open floor plan.

Of course, the front door was locked. Someone had left a single light burning somewhere down the hall. She had to be content with peering through a window.

The hardwood floors gleamed. In the front foyer, a set of stairs led upward to the second floor. Did Hutch have plans to settle down and fill his new home with children and a wife?

A wide porch ran all the way around the main floor of the house. It would be perfect for swings and flowerpots and maybe even a hammock on the side facing away from the street. She sat on the back steps and propped her hands behind her. The night breeze picked up, raising gooseflesh on her arms beneath the light sweater.

Hutch had clearly come home to Royal planning to stay. He'd been awarded a prestigious job, and he had family nearby. Everything he could possibly want, Royal had to offer.

It would be up to Simone to learn how to be friendly without betraying her secret. Hutch could never know she still loved him.

Moodily, she kicked at a cricket that hopped around her shoe. "Go away," she said. "I don't like pests."

"I hope that doesn't mean me."

The deep voice startled her. She jumped to her feet, and as she did so, her toe caught the edge of the top step. She pitched forward in slow motion, striking her knee hard on the wooden floor of the porch.

Hutch reached for her, but she went all the way down in an ungainly heap. Pain shot from her shin to her toe.

"Did you hit your head?" he asked urgently, squatting beside her as she struggled to sit up.

"No."

"Are you sure?"

She gaped at him. "Seriously? You don't even think I'm capable of assessing my own injuries?"

"Do you have a medical degree?" he asked mildly.

Refusing to admit that her leg hurt like hell, she shook her head. "No, Doctor, I don't. I can tell you with confidence, though, I'm fine."

He helped her to her feet. "What are you doing at my house?"

That was a tricky question. He didn't sound mad, but he didn't come across as friendly, either.

"I couldn't sleep."

"So you thought breaking and entering was the way to go?"

Thirteen

Hutch was stunned at how glad he was to see her. The last twenty-four hours had been rough. He'd been forced to rethink his whole life's plan. And all because of an impetuous, contrary, completely frustrating woman who was pregnant with another man's babies.

Simone's grin was sheepish. "I was curious about your house."

"Would you like a tour?"

"Of course."

He unlocked the front door, feeling the same rush of satisfaction that had overwhelmed him when he signed his name on the sheaf of closing papers. This old house welcomed him. Though he wasn't a whimsical man, he had a healthy respect for the past. He liked feeling a part of something bigger than he was.

He led Simone from room to room, standing back and observing as she got to know his home.

In the dining room, she ran her hand along the chair rail. "It's beautiful, Hutch. The whole place. I can imagine Christmas dinners in this room."

The dining room was larger than most. It included a working fireplace that would be expensive to insure and maintain, but Hutch looked forward to using it the following winter. "I have some painting to do. And a few small repairs. Hopefully, I'll be able to move in a couple of weeks from now."

She stood at the window, looking out into the dark with her back to him. "Why such a big place, Hutch?"

The silence lasted for half a dozen beats. "The usual reasons. I want to have a family someday…a boring, normal life."

She glanced at him over her shoulder. "You'll never be boring, trust me. Arrogant, maybe. Bossy, infuriating and egotistical. But not boring."

"Careful, Simone. Too many compliments and I'll begin to think you might actually like me."

She whirled around. "Those *weren't* compliments, Dr. Hutchinson."

He chuckled. "Come on. I'll show you the kitchen." Actually, it was the kitchen that had sold him on the house. All the modern conveniences were included, but the hardwood floor remained, as well as the antique oak cabinets. During past renovations, granite countertops had been chosen to complement the color of the wood. Cream appliances, clearly special ordered, finished the cozy look.

Simone put her hands to her cheeks. "Oh, Hutch. This is gorgeous."

Her reaction pleased him more than it should. "I'm glad you like it. My parents raised me to appreciate the old with the new. I made an offer on this place the first time I saw it. I knew it was the one for me."

Without overthinking it, he put his hands on Simone's waist and lifted her to sit on the countertop. "I owe you an apology," he said.

"For what?" Her gaze was wary.

"For thinking it was my right to go with you to the ultrasound. You're a grown woman. Those babies you carry are your responsibility. I was out of line." He had realized his mistake after storming out of Simone's house. As much as he hated to admit it, she had been right to go alone.

"It went well," Simone said, her soft smile radiant. "Dr. Fetter says I have three viable fetuses. Three babies, Hutch. Can you imagine? Not one, but three. I don't know whether to be terrified or ecstatic."

"A little of both would be in order." He kissed her forehead. "I have a question to ask you."

Her eyes widened. "What is it?"

"Would you allow me the honor of escorting you to the masquerade ball?" He'd been thinking about it on and off. He realized there was no other man he'd want to see by her side. Even the thought of it left a bad taste in his mouth. In his gut, he knew he was cruising for a fall, yet he was helpless to stop himself.

Knowing the right thing and doing it were two entirely different realities.

Simone nodded slowly. "I like that idea. In fact, I was going to ask *you*, but you beat me to it." She hooked two fingers in the open neckline of his collar and pulled. "Let's seal the deal."

One thing he'd always loved about Simone was her confidence when it came to sex. She had a healthy self-

image, and she didn't play coy games. "I could be per-
suaded," he muttered. Already, his body responded to
her invitation. He was pretty sure all she had in mind
was a kiss. Still, he was good at persuasion.

With a deep sigh that encompassed relief and in-
evitability, he slid his hands beneath her hair and
cupped her face. "You are so damned beautiful, Simone Parker. I think pregnancy becomes you."

It was the hint of vulnerability in her blue eyes that
did him in. It always had. He kissed her slowly, taking
his time, demanding a response and receiving more
than he asked in return.

Her arms wrapped around his neck in a strangle-
hold. "Let's declare a truce," she pleaded in between
frantic kisses. "Until after the babies are born."

"On what grounds?" He nipped her bottom lip with
his teeth. She had put him through hell over the years.
It was only reasonable that he made her work for this.

"Neighbors. Friendship. Old times."

"I could live with that. Lift your hips, woman."

When she obeyed instantly, dangerous lust roared
through his veins. He ripped her jeans down her legs
and tossed them aside. Her white cotton undies struck
him as ridiculously erotic. Pressing two fingertips to
her center, he caressed her through the layer of fabric.

Simone gasped, arching her back. He lifted her
sweater but didn't take the time to remove it completely. Then he went still. "You're not wearing a bra."

As statements went, that one was sophomoric at
best. But his brain had gone all fuzzy. "You're not
wearing a bra," he repeated, dumbfounded.

Simone cocked her head and gave him an impertinent smile. "It's late. I was all alone. I had no idea the master of the house was planning to seduce me."

"I wasn't planning *anything*," he insisted. "But when a man finds a gift on his porch, he isn't dumb enough to throw it away." Deliberately taking his time, he lowered the zipper on his pants.

Simone shivered. "Are there any beds upstairs?"

"Not even a measly cot. Don't worry, little mama. We'll make do."

"Hurry," she said.

When the tail of his shirt caught in his zipper, Simone laughed. "For a doctor, you're awfully clumsy."

She was taunting him deliberately. It was an old game they played, one guaranteed to drive him insane. At last he managed to free his erection. He was burning up, but a shiver snaked its way down his spine as he looked at his very first houseguest.

"We can do this," he muttered. Somehow.

Simone scooted closer to the edge of the counter. "That refrigerator seems awfully sturdy."

"Good point." He lifted her into his arms and groaned when she wrapped her legs around his waist and her arms around his neck.

"You won't be able to do this too much longer," Simone said.

"Couples can have sex until very late in the pregnancy." He was counting on it.

"I was talking about carrying me, silly man. But I like where you're headed."

Where he was headed was to a padded room if he didn't get inside her soon. "Hold on," he muttered. He pushed her up against the refrigerator and grinned when the cold metal against her bum made her squeak.

"I hope you're not attached to this underwear." Panting from exertion, he kept one arm around his prize and used his free hand to shove aside the narrow strip of fabric that was the only thing standing in his way.

When he joined their bodies, Simone moaned and buried her face in his neck. "Oh, Hutch."

He loved the way she said his name, her bedroom voice drowsy with pleasure. Simone could be a firecracker, a sharp-edged combatant. But when he had her like this, she was an entirely different person.

"Hold on, darlin'," he said, barely able to form a coherent sentence. The position taxed his strength, but it also gave him a jolt of satisfaction. Slowly, steadily, he thrust upward, taking her again and again until there was nothing left to take.

In this position, Simone was helpless. He was the aggressor. If there had been anything on top of the fridge, it would have crashed to the floor. He thrust wildly, coming in a climax so powerful it blurred his vision.

Through it all, Simone clung to him and never let go.

At last, the storm passed. He thought he heard and felt her orgasm. He hoped so. In his own delirium, he hadn't been the most considerate of lovers.

He eased her to her feet and steadied her when her legs wobbled. The water had been turned on, so the kitchen tap worked. There was nothing in the house, though. No paper napkins, no cloth towels.

Simone wrinkled her nose. "I should go home now. I need a shower. And it's late."

He nodded. "You want some company?"

She looked up at him, smaller and less combative than in many of their confrontations. Her smile bloomed, her blue eyes clear and happy. "What a lovely idea, Dr. Hutchinson."

That first evening set the tone for days that followed. He and Simone, by unspoken agreement, tabled their arguments and their differences. Often, he slept at her place. Other nights he worked at his own home, unpacking boxes until his eyes crossed with exhaustion. Simone tried to help, but he'd been forced to exile her when he found her lifting a container of heavy glassware in the kitchen. She'd pouted at him, but she hadn't gotten mad.

They were living in a fantasy world, totally ignoring the fact that Simone's life was about to change radically. Not to mention his.

Once the triplets were born, he wouldn't see much of Simone anymore. She would have her hands full caring for three small infants.

The thought of losing her again made his stomach clench. He reminded himself that he hadn't been home from Sudan long. Royal had dozens of available women, one of whom might even be his soul mate if he believed in such a thing. He was a man in his prime. During med school, he hadn't sown many wild oats. He'd been focused on getting through and excelling. It was what his parents expected and what Hutch wanted.

Now was the perfect time in his life to see who was out there for him. Not that he was foolish enough to think that there was another woman who could set his blood on fire like Simone did—but a man could hope.

Fortunately, Simone was incredibly busy getting things ready for the masquerade ball. He didn't have to worry about neglecting her when things got crazy at the hospital. The advent of the full moon meant a rush of babies being born. Though he hadn't picked up many patients of his own yet, he'd been called in on several high-risk cases.

A breech birth. One drug-addicted newborn. A seven-month infant delivered prematurely as a result of a car accident. Thankfully, in that situation, mother and baby had stabilized, but it was touch and go for a while.

There were seventy-two straight hours where Hutch didn't make it home at all. He snatched a few hours of sleep in the doctors' lounge, but it was fragmented rest and unsatisfying. He lived off hospital food and bottled water. The only way he knew time had passed was that he changed into clean scrubs twice a day.

Several times he thought about texting Simone, but each moment he pulled out his phone, he ended up being summoned to one labor room or another.

His week went from bad to worse on Wednesday. A young woman, barely six months pregnant and a recent transplant to Royal, came in through the ER. Her vitals were all over the map and the monitors showed fetal distress. It took hours, but finally a team nailed down the cause. The woman was diagnosed with a previously undetected and very rare blood abnormality. She was hemorrhaging internally.

Despite every attempt to save them, the mother and baby both died.

Unfortunately, Hutch's on-call rotation ended on that note. What he desperately wanted was to stay at the hospital and lose himself in work, trying to get those images out of his head. But that choice would endanger the patients in his care because of his extreme exhaustion.

Instead, he would do the mature, responsible thing. He would go home and sleep.

Simone bounced from day to day on a bubble of pure happiness. All of her problems were still out there on the horizon, but for now, life was good.

The masquerade party appeared destined to be a smashing success. Over 95 percent of the invitees had responded with an enthusiastic yes.

Thanks to Simone and her staff, the event received unprecedented saturation in both traditional print media and radio as well as blogs, email blasts and social media. Naomi and Cecelia had coordinated an entire crew of volunteers to help transform the ballroom. Tomorrow, the actual decorations would start going up.

Every day, Simone tried on the red dress, almost superstitiously afraid to leave anything to chance. She'd heard some pregnant women say they'd had to resort to maternity clothes overnight. One day they were fine with their jeans unzipped, the next, nothing fit.

She didn't want that to happen to her.

Knowing that Hutch would be her date for the party was both exciting and alarming. Even with Hutch wearing a mask, everyone would know who he was. Then the speculation would begin.

It probably already had, but this would be the first and likely only time she and Hutch would make an official appearance as a couple. Simone was pregnant. Hutch was back from Africa. Lots of people would make educated guesses.

She hadn't heard a word from him in almost four

days. Fortunately, she wasn't the kind of woman who needed constant attention from a man. Still, when he neither texted nor called, she began to wonder if she had done something to upset him.

Though she was feeling markedly more like herself, Dr. Fetter had been insistent that Simone not overdo it. Thus, even though Thursday would be the last full workday before the party, Simone closed the office at five sharp on Wednesday and drove herself home.

Now that she felt like eating again—at least most of the time—she was actually hungry. Would Hutch be up for dinner at a quiet restaurant? Honestly, that sounded wonderful to Simone. This pregnancy was taking more of a toll on her body than she had anticipated. Her usual fount of energy was nowhere to be seen. Unwinding with Hutch and a nice, juicy steak might perk her up.

On a whim, she texted him before getting in the shower. By the time she was clean and dry and dressed, he still hadn't answered. Frowning, she tried to recall his schedule. She was almost certain he'd said he'd be off on Thursday *and* Friday, which meant that his shift should have ended this afternoon.

Maybe she would pick up carryout Chinese and go over to his house. If he was tired, too, he might welcome the food and the company. At one time, she would have been reluctant to invade his privacy. They'd been on good terms lately, though.

She sent him another text.

Still, he did not answer.

Bit by bit, her confidence eroded. She and Hutch were temporary. They both acknowledged that. What if Hutch had met someone else? What if he regretted his offer to escort her to the masquerade ball?

Maybe he and the mystery woman were over at his house now christening Hutch's new bed. He'd been sleeping on a mattress on the floor, but she had met the furniture delivery truck day before yesterday and opened Hutch's house so the men could set up the massive cherry king-size bed in the master suite.

Even with misgivings swirling in her stomach, she grabbed her keys and climbed into the car. Unfortunately, the Chinese restaurant was in the wrong direction, but the detour gave her more time to think. The order took no time at all. When she arrived at Hutch's place, the house was dark, and his car was in the driveway.

Now, she began to get worried. What if he were ill?

That was dumb. The man was a doctor. He was more than capable of taking care of himself.

Again, she wondered if his sudden absence from her life was because he had realized he was wasting his time. The man had a strongly developed moral conscience. Perhaps it had finally occurred to him that Simone was not meant to be a part of his life.

Leaving the food in her car for the moment, she got out and walked up the front steps. Testing the door gingerly, she found it locked.

Maybe he had come home and gone to bed early. At six forty-five? Not likely. Then what was the explanation for the fact that the house was in total darkness? Again, her mind went to the other-woman theory. If Hutch had brought someone home with him, they could be upstairs.

With her chest tight, she took a deep breath and let

it out. Hutch would never sleep with two women at the same time. If he met someone else, he would do the honorable thing and tell Simone face-to-face.

Even so, she had a bad feeling about this. Something was definitely amiss. Had the blackmailer chosen now as the time to reveal Simone's secret? Was Hutch pondering how to boot her out of his life?

She had to *make* herself walk around the porch. The easy thing would be to run away. But she had to be sure Hutch was okay.

The end of her search was anticlimactic. She found him sitting on the top step, slumped over, his elbows on his knees, his head in his hand.

"Hutch?" She crouched beside him, alarmed. Something in his body language kept her from touching him. "Why didn't you answer my texts?"

"Go home, Simone."

She froze. His voice was monotone, gruff and raspy. "Have I done something to offend you, Hutch? Talk to me. I can't fix it if you don't let me know what it is."

He stood up, forcing her to do the same. His eyes were the dull brown of fallen leaves in the late fall. Yet somehow, a tiny flame in them seared her. His body language spoke volumes. "For God's sake, Simone. The whole damn world doesn't revolve around you. Not everything I do or don't do is about *you*. Grow up, damn it. I don't need you hovering every minute of every day."

Fourteen

Simone gaped at him, her heart imploding in shock and bitter hurt. Never, even in their most painful days before he left for Sudan, had Hutch lashed out like this. He'd always possessed a maturity beyond his years. Hutch was never cruel.

Apparently, people changed.

She could do nothing about the tears that spilled down her cheeks. Stepping back awkwardly, unconsciously putting distance between herself and the furious, aggressive male, she held out a hand. "I shouldn't have come. My mistake."

Hutch only stared at her.

Everything crumbled in slow motion. The faux happiness that had helped her ignore their problems was a sham. She'd been living in a dream world.

One last time, she tried to get through to him. "I

brought dinner. Chinese. Your favorite. I'll grab it from the car."

"I'm not hungry. And I'm not in the mood for company."

"I see." She didn't. Not at all. But she wasn't stupid. "Okay, then." Embarrassed, humiliated, hurt and angry, she gave him a curt nod. Without another word, she fled.

It took her three tries to put the car into gear. She was crying so hard, she couldn't see. At the end of Hutch's driveway, she stopped. She shouldn't operate a vehicle in her condition. Resting her head on the steering wheel, she wept.

Hutch had taken a bad day and made it worse. In the midst of his burning guilt and regret over what had happened at the hospital, he had added the poisonous taste of shame. The memory of Simone's face galvanized him into action.

Racing around the side of the house, he inhaled sharply when he saw her car still parked in his driveway. He jerked open the driver's-side door and felt like the lowest kind of scum when he realized she was crying too hard to make the short trip home.

"Oh, hell," he groaned. "Come here, baby. I'm a bastard. Let me hold you."

He scooped her out of the car without a struggle. Bumping the door closed with his hip, he strode back to the house.

Inside, he wasted no time. He carried her up the stairs and sat down with her on his bed. "I'm sorry, Simone. My bad temper had nothing to do with you. Please forgive me."

She had cried so hard her face was blotchy and red. And she couldn't stop. He held her tightly, unable to stem the flow of tears.

It was a hell of a time to figure out he was still in love with her.

The bolt of truth was a knife to his gut. Was this something new, or had his feelings for Simone lain dormant all those years in Sudan? Maybe deep down, his guilt over Bethany's death wasn't so much about not being able to save her as it was knowing he had never loved her the way he should have.

Bethany had given her heart and her trust to him. Had he unwittingly offered her far less in return?

He stroked Simone's hair. "Hush now. You'll make yourself sick again."

It took a long time, but finally, Simone wore herself out.

He wiped her face with the tail of his shirt. To explain would be to dump some of his anguish on her, but how else could he account for being so deliberately cruel? "I lost a mother and a baby today," he muttered. It embarrassed him that his voice broke on the word *baby*.

Simone struggled to sit up. She stared at him with big, wet eyes. "Oh, Hutch. What happened?"

He gave her an abbreviated version. "I don't think the patient ever really had a chance, but we tried. God, we tried. I kept seeing the nurses' faces. It's hard, you know. We're supposed to maintain that professional distance…so we can do what we have to do. Loss of life in any circumstance is difficult beyond words. This…this was devastating."

"The baby couldn't be saved?"

"No. She looked perfect. Tiny, but perfect. Still, it was far too soon. Sometimes, even with all our sophisticated equipment and technology, we can't overcome that. We save dozens of preemies, often against large odds. Today we lost. She lived for an hour."

Simone—generous, openhearted Simone—wrapped her arms around him and held him so tightly he could barely breathe. Or maybe that was his reaction to knowing he had the love of his life in his arms.

She shuddered. "I can't even imagine what it was like for all of you. I couldn't do what you do. How does anyone bear it?"

He *knew* what she was thinking. "You don't have to worry about your pregnancy, Simone. The woman today had a serious medical condition. You're healthy and strong and perfectly normal."

"I don't think anyone's ever called me normal." Her smile was wry, her face still damp as she pulled back and stared at him.

He wanted to ease her down on the bed and make love to her to erase the memories of the day. But he felt raw and unsteady and light-headed. It was a time for caution. Simone didn't deserve to be used as tranquilizer. He needed to take stock of what was happening.

Carefully, he released her and stood up. "Did you mention something about food?" he asked, trying to lighten the mood.

Simone's face was hard to read. She rose as well, her posture defensive, arms wrapped tightly around her waist. And no wonder. He'd treated her like dirt. She shrugged. "It's hot outside. I don't know if we should risk it. Food poisoning is not fun."

He winced. "True." And in Simone's condition, it

could be lethal. "What if we drive through somewhere and grab a milk shake and fries?"

She raised an eyebrow. "For a doctor, you don't seem to have a grasp of good nutrition."

He knew she was teasing him. "After today, I think we could both use some junk food, don't you? How about it?"

Simone hesitated. "I need to get home," she said.

"You're mad."

"No." She shook her head vehemently. "I forgive you. But the next two days are going to be tough. Dr. Fetter says I need to pace myself."

"Of course." He didn't want to eat alone. He sure as hell didn't want to sleep alone. But his outburst on the back porch had changed something. Maybe Simone was rethinking her relationship with him.

The awkward conversation ended there. Simone headed downstairs with him on her heels. Once she climbed into her car and started the engine, he leaned down, one hand on top of the car. "Are you sure you're okay to drive?"

Simone nodded. "I'm good."

He winced, remembering what else he had to tell her. "I'd hoped to do something fun with you tomorrow, but my dad needs me to help him in the garden. The man does love his fresh produce, but he over-planted his year."

"No worries, Hutch." Her gaze was guarded. "I'm going to be working flat out, too. I'll see you Friday evening."

"What time do you want me to pick you up?"

"Five thirty will work. I have to be there early. I

could drive my own car, though," she said. "No need for you to hang around."

"I could help."

She pursed her lips. "Maybe. What if I let you know tomorrow?"

"I'm picking you up, Simone. End of discussion." His temper started a slow boil. Something had shifted. Was it the things he had said to her earlier? Had he damaged a relationship already on shaky ground? Or was something else going on?

"Fine." Simone revved the engine. "Good night, Hutch."

He was forced to step back or risk having her run over his foot. After his recent behavior, he couldn't blame her.

Simone refused to think about Dr. Troy Hutchinson. He could hurt her only if she allowed it. The new lives growing in her womb were all she needed. Even if Hutch wanted to hang around after the babies came, she wouldn't have time for him.

Tonight had exposed a valuable truth. Hutch didn't love her. It hurt to admit it. It hurt like hell. But she was better off accepting reality.

She didn't hold his bad temper against him. Anyone in a similar situation would be raw and grief stricken and likely to lash out. No, that wasn't the root of her sadness. What pained her was that Hutch, in his hour of need, hadn't turned to Simone for help and comfort. If she dug deep to the heart of their relationship, she saw the chasm between what she wanted and what he was willing to give her.

Friendship? Yes. They had mended fences over

their earlier breakup and moved on. Sex? The sex was amazing…hot, intense and deeply satisfying. She and Hutch had no problems in the bedroom.

She could even see that the two of them had established a tentative relationship of trust. Certainly, she trusted him to look after her physical well-being. Not only that, but Hutch had been very honest with her about Bethany. There were very few secrets between them.

Though in Simone's case, the one she had omitted was gigantic.

Tonight's drama with Hutch had stolen her appetite, replacing it with the now-familiar nausea. Nursing a cup of hot tea, she curled up in the comfy chair in her bedroom and opened her laptop.

For some reason, she had never deleted the message from the mysterious Maverick. The cryptic note was evidence, in any case. Maybe he or she was not a threat anymore. Word of her pregnancy was slowly beginning to spread. The cat was out of the bag. Perhaps Maverick had wanted to extort money from her to keep her pregnancy quiet.

When she opened Facebook, she saw that she had received a new message. She clicked on it and read, "Your day of reckoning is near. Maverick."

That was odd. And menacing. She placed a hand on her stomach, instinctively alarmed. It was one thing to fear for her own safety. Now she carried the responsibility for three tiny humans.

The only secret she had kept from Hutch and her friends…from everyone, in fact, was private. This Maverick person would have no reason to know what Simone had done…or at least *why* she had done it.

She hated feeling helpless. Even more, she hated feeling powerless to track down the subpar person who held grudges against so many of Royal's upstanding citizens. She sure as heck wasn't going to engage in an online conversation with Maverick. The best thing to do was to go about her business, pretending that everything was normal.

Thursday morning dawned bright and clear and sunny. After a restless sleep, Simone was grateful for weather that lifted her spirits. Sometime around three the night before, she had turned on the light and made a list. She was a mother-to-be with a successful business to run.

This thing with Hutch, well, it was fun, but it was also painful. After tomorrow night, it was probably best if she put an end to it. At least that way, she would be the one calling the shots and not Hutch.

Beneath her surface calm, her heart was breaking. She wanted it all. The babies. The company she had built from the ground up. The respect of her parents. And last but not least, she wanted the man she had loved since she was twenty-two years old.

Fifty percent wasn't a bad average. In baseball, it was extraordinary. Too bad she had never been good at sports.

After showering and drying her hair, she put on a new black knit dress and topped it with a cheery hot-pink cardigan. The knit fabric and empire waistline were designed to grow along with her belly. Today, it simply looked liked a casual outfit suited to a pleasant spring day.

She had called Tess and told her she was coming in a little late. Tess was brilliant. Simone had hired the younger woman straight out of business school with a freshly minted MBA. At no time had Tess ever let her down or not been able to handle the work. Simone was counting on that.

When she made it in to her office, she asked Tess to come in and close the door. Tess might have been alarmed, but she didn't show it. "What's up, boss?"

Simone had insisted that Tess call her by her first name. But Tess had just as insistently refused. Simone eyed the girl on the other side of the desk. From her magenta-accented pixie cut to her triple-pierced right ear, Tess was an original.

For some reason, Simone was having a hard time getting this conversation off the ground. "Tess," she said, "are you happy working with me?"

Tess nodded. "Of course."

"And do you have plans to move up the ladder? To go somewhere else? Dallas, maybe? Or Houston?"

"None." A tiny frown appeared between Tess's brows. "Are you trying to get rid of me?"

"Not at all. Quite the opposite."

"I'm confused."

Simone realized she wasn't handling this well. "I suppose you know I'm pregnant."

Tess grimaced. "Yes, ma'am."

"What you may not know is that I'm having triplets."

"Good God." Tess's eyes rounded. "I hope it's not contagious." She shuddered. "I'm not antibaby, but three?"

"Yeah," Simone said wryly. "It's a lot to take in. But on the other hand, it's a done deal, so I'm trying to make plans."

"No offense, boss, but I'm not really a fan of little kids. They scare me. Probably comes from my dad dropping me on my head when I was six months old. I think it warped me."

Tess was talking a mile a minute, clearly rattled.

Simone sighed. "Stand down, Tess. I'm not asking you to babysit. I want to know if you're willing to be top dog of this company for a year. I'd still be involved in all major decisions, but you would be in charge. What do you think?"

"Where will you be?"

"At home. I'll have help with the triplets...out of necessity. There's no way I can do it alone. But I'll be their mother. Even saying that out loud sounds strange. I want these babies, Tess. I'm going to give this motherhood thing a hundred percent of my time when they're born, at least for a year. After that, if we've managed some kind of routine, I may consider day care. But that's a long time off, so I can't think about that now."

"You're awfully brave."

"Not brave. Just determined. If you need time to think about this, I understand."

"I don't have to think about it," Tess said with a huge grin. "I'm honored. And pumped. You can count on me, boss."

"When we get around to this new arrangement, do you think you could call me Simone?"

Tess shrugged sheepishly. "Maybe. I'll try."

"Good. And, Tess?"

"Yes, ma'am?"

"This is between you and me for the next few

months. I don't want anyone to know I'm thinking about taking a sabbatical. It's my business."

"I get it." She mimed sealing her lips. "Your secrets will go to my grave."

"Thank you." Simone shooed her out and tackled the stack of paperwork overflowing her inbox. Between snail mail and email, she never caught up. The business was growing undeniably. Soon, she might have to consider adding another employee. But then again, with Simone gone for a year, they might lose ground. It would be a game of wait and see.

For the second day in a row, she closed the office at five. As someone accustomed to keeping late hours when in the midst of a project, it was not her usual behavior. She liked to think motherhood was going to be good for her. Keeping a healthier lifestyle...all of that.

She didn't call Hutch that evening. Or text him.

He didn't contact her, either. Maybe they were both ready to admit their relationship was never going to blossom into something permanent. Simone had known that from the beginning. Getting pregnant with an unknown man's sperm had erased virtually every chance she had to get married. No one she knew would be willing to take on a young mom with three babies, even if that man was madly in love with her.

Hutch wasn't madly in love. She didn't deceive herself there. He liked her. He enjoyed having regular sex. Neither of those things guaranteed a happily-ever-after. As she let herself into the house, she told herself she could handle this baby thing with or without Hutch.

Though she cooked oatmeal for dinner, she was barely able to eat half. Afterward, she read and watched TV until ten o'clock. Like a high school girl in the throes of a crush, she picked up her phone every ten seconds to check for messages.

The screen remained blank.

Uncertainty was painful and demoralizing. She was even more resolved to end things with Hutch after the ball. Never mind that her heart raced in panic at the thought. The two of them had enjoyed reuniting. Nothing that came afterward pointed to a rosy future. Even Hutch himself had never made any pretense of wanting to be a father to her babies. He was too honest to lead her astray.

More honest than she deserved.

When she finally turned out the light and curled up in a ball underneath the covers, her heart raced. Tomorrow night was big. Huge, in fact. A good turnout meant significant sums of money for the charity.

Unfortunately, all she cared about at the moment was seeing Hutch again and, hopefully, dancing the night away. Even if the bliss would only be temporary.

Fifteen

Hutch had some big decisions to make. He knew it, but he couldn't quite wrap his head around what that would mean. Everyone thought he was so smart, so damned wise. The truth was, he was as clueless as the next guy.

It felt odd to put on a tux again. He'd been forced to buy a new one for the masquerade ball. His time in Africa had made him leaner, harder. Living life on the edge of civilization had taught him how to survive without many of the comforts of home. His physical stamina was greater than it had ever been.

He looked at himself in the mirror and straightened his bow tie with a grimace. All he had ever wanted in life was to make his parents proud of him. On a whim, he grabbed his keys and headed out to the car. It was too early to pick up Simone, but he had a sudden urge to see his father.

Both his parents were sitting outside on the porch enjoying a cold beer when Hutch arrived. His mother was her usual stately, put-together self. His dad was scruffy today. Apparently, he'd worked in the garden again.

Hutch took a wicker chair and sat across from them.

His mother cocked her head. "Did I forget it's my birthday? You look very handsome this evening, Hutch."

The senior Hutchinson nodded. "You clean up real nice. But I'm guessing you didn't come to pull more weeds."

"Should I leave you two boys alone?" his mother asked.

"No, ma'am." Hutch might be closing in on his midthirties, but his mother still ruled their family with an iron fist. "I want you both to hear this."

"So serious," she said, smiling. But he noted a trace of anxiety in her brown eyes that were so like his.

His father frowned. "Spit it out, son. Bad news never gets any better in the waiting."

"Who said I have bad news?" Hutch ran a hand over his head, aware that he was starting to sweat.

His mother leaned forward and patted his knee. "You look as somber as a judge. Tell us, son."

Hutch rubbed his damp palms on his pants legs. "Do you remember Simone Parker?"

Both of the older adults flinched. "We do," his father said. "Your grandmother never got over the way she treated you. Thank God she's passed on. I have a feeling she wouldn't like what you're about to tell us."

"You raised me to believe that people deserve second chances."

"Yes, we did," his mother said. "But that woman was wrong for you in many ways."

Hutch bristled. "Like what? I thought you were glad she convinced me to go to Sudan."

His dad drained his beer and set the bottle on the floor. "We were. We still are. Those years will make a huge difference in how you practice medicine. But this Simone…well, she's…" He trailed off.

"She's selfish and shallow," his mother said sharply. "She has a reputation around town as a bit of a snob. Only child. Wealthy parents."

"I'm an only child," Hutch pointed out mildly, though he felt anything but calm. "I'm surprised to hear both of you speak so negatively. Simone might have been a little self-centered in her youth, but she's changed."

His father shrugged. "If you've come to ask for our blessing, I don't think we can offer it. But you're a grown man and long past needing our approval. Give it some time, boy. Sleep with her, but don't marry her."

Hutch's mother punched her husband in the arm… hard. "Don't talk like that, Edward Hutchinson. What's gotten into you?"

"You don't like her, either."

"I don't know her," she conceded.

Hutch stood up. He wasn't sure what he had expected from his parents. Maybe he just wanted someone to tell him that what he was contemplating wouldn't make a damn fool out of him. "I haven't made any big decisions, so you can quit having heart attacks. I suppose I was hoping you'd tell me that true love lasts."

"Well, of course it does," his father said. "The trick is to marry the right person in the first place."

Hutch was not in a good frame of mind to go to a party. He was horny and agitated and completely confused. Just when he thought he had things figured out, something happened. Either Simone pulled back, or he did. And now his parents, thanks to him, had weighed in on the situation. With a big ol' negative.

He parked in Simone's driveway and stared up at the house. The structure was attractive and neatly kept. Exactly like its owner. The golden brick with the mahogany shutters at the windows was modern and, at the same time, classic.

Fumbling to slide his phone into his pocket, he told himself that tonight was not the time for grand gestures. Tonight was mostly business for Simone. He was only her escort, not her boyfriend. In fact, this wasn't some romantic date where the two of them would be all alone.

Two-thirds or more of Royal's movers and shakers would be out in force tonight. Maybe they would come to show off their jewels and their trophy wives. Perhaps they really cared about the charity. Either way, the word of the evening was *money*…and lots of it.

Simone answered the door as soon as he knocked. He took a step backward, feeling a mule kick to the chest. She looked incredible.

"Hi, Hutch," she said breathlessly. "Come on in. I'm almost ready. A phone call slowed me down."

She was fluttering, nervous, her eyes not quite meeting his.

Without overthinking it, Hutch captured her wrist and gently reeled her in. "You look stunning, Simone." He kissed her softly, keeping a tight check on his cave-man instincts. Her lips were soft beneath his. Her hands landed on his shoulders. For a few breath-stealing moments, he lost himself in the kiss. He wanted to carry her up the stairs and lock the door.

His heart pounded, his entire body hard as iron. He wanted to take and take and take. The prospect of sharing her with hundreds of other people tonight was unappealing at best.

She wore a red dress designed to make a statement. Simone Parker was *in* the building. In his arms she felt fragile and small, though he knew she was anything but. Simone was smart and strong and determined. Having triplets would be extremely challenging, but he had no doubts about her ability to cope.

In the end, he had to force himself to release her and step back. Her silky black hair fell in soft waves about her shoulders. Her sapphire eyes, framed in dark lashes, sparkled.

Her grin was self-conscious. "I really do have to finish getting ready."

He waved a hand. "Go. I'll entertain myself down here." He glanced at his watch. "You'd better hurry, though, if we're supposed to be getting there early."

Simone rolled her eyes. "I'm not the one who started that kiss."

She disappeared before he could retaliate. With a smile on his face, he prowled the downstairs restlessly.

Anticipation flooded his veins. He and Simone had things to discuss. Big things. Life-changing things. Maybe this time, they could rewrite the ending.

After the talk with Tess, Simone had begun to feel as if she finally had a handle on the mess that was her life. Seeing Hutch at her door just now in black tie knocked the wind out of her. He was so handsome, so brilliant, so unbelievably sexy. Why would a man like that want to tie himself to a woman like Simone? Nevertheless, she was going to give it a shot.

She had built her business on taking calculated risks. Hutch cared about her. The fact that he wanted her physically was irrefutable. The only question that remained was how he would respond if Simone asked for more.

Earlier, she had decided to break things off with Hutch, but that was the coward's way out. Tonight, after the ball, she was going to lay her cards on the table. Love was a hard thing to offer outright, but maybe she owed him that. Above all, she was going to confess the truth. It would put her in a bad light, no doubt about it. Still, there was no hope for a future with Hutch unless she was completely honest.

After tweaking her hair one last time and applying a bold lipstick to match her dress, she eyed her reflection in the long mirror on the back of her closet door. Not too shabby. She placed her hand, palm flat, against her belly. Feeling the tiny bulge filled her with wonder and humility.

Despite everything she had done wrong in her life, here was a chance for a new start. More than anything else, she wanted to be a good mother to these three babies. Unlike her own upbringing, she was determined to be a hands-on parent. Though she would have to have help, professional or otherwise, she was going to be *present*.

A quick glance at the clock told her there was no time left to linger. Lifting her skirt in one hand, she made her way carefully down the stairs. Hutch stood at the bottom, waiting. She held up a hand. "No more kissing. I'm camera ready, as Naomi would say."

His smile was wicked. "I can wait. Maybe." He ran his thumb over her cheekbone. "Let's just say I'm really looking forward to removing that dress in a few hours."

"Hutch!" She gaped at him.

He shrugged. "If you don't want me to open the gift, you shouldn't wrap it so nicely."

They made it to the hotel in record time. Because they were early, traffic wasn't bad yet. In the parking lot, Simone handed Hutch the rectangular box that had come in the mail. "These are our masks. Will you hang on to them for the moment?"

He grimaced, exhibiting the usual male reluctance for such things. "Sure."

The following hour was taken up with a variety of last-minute responsibilities. While Hutch cooled his heels in the bar, Simone met with Naomi and Cecelia for one final, excited rundown. Everything had fallen into place perfectly.

At last, it was time to find Hutch and start enjoying the more personal portion of the evening. He had returned to the car in search of fresh air and his business card wallet. After a quick text to ascertain his whereabouts, she joined him there, relishing the moment of privacy inside the vehicle to catch her breath and collect her thoughts before the event began in earnest. "I missed you, my handsome doctor."

As masquerade parties went, this one was going to be ultrasophisticated, no costumes or elaborate ensembles allowed. The men had been instructed to wear traditional tuxes. With so many of them in the room, anonymity would be upheld. The women, on the other hand, had been asked to choose a color. The masks for the female guests would complement their gowns. Simone's mask was scarlet trimmed with delicate black lace.

Her heart beat faster when Hutch put on his black mask. It made him look remote and dangerous. "Will you help me with mine?" she said. "So I won't mess up my hair?"

Hutch took the mask from her trembling fingers and carefully fitted it over her head, smoothing any strands of hair that were pushed out of place. Then he bared the side of her neck and pressed a kiss just below her ear. "I could eat you alive," he muttered.

His hot breath against her skin and the subtle rake of his teeth against her sensitive flesh flooded her body with heat and yearning. "I could say the same to you," she whispered. "I used to think your white lab coat was the sexiest piece of clothing you owned. But tonight you're seriously hot. I'll have my hands full keeping other women from stealing you away."

He cupped his hand around her breast, using his thumb to tease the nipple that beaded beneath the fabric. "Does that mean you want me all to yourself?"

Simone shuddered. Arousal stole through her veins

and made her reckless. "I dare anyone to lay a hand on you, Troy Hutchinson. For tonight, you're mine."

He groaned, resting his forehead against hers. "What are we doing, damn it? I can't walk in there with an erection. Hell, Simone, you make me crazy."

For once, he didn't sound too happy about that. She sat back in her seat and tried to steady her breathing. "I'll go in alone," she said. "You can follow when you're ready."

Beneath the mask, his jaw was like iron. "I'm ready now," he growled, deliberately misunderstanding her suggestion. The words were forced beneath clenched teeth.

Helpless to stem the tide of insanity that had overtaken them, she touched him lightly through his trousers. His erection was as hard as his jaw. "Oh, Hutch," she said. "What I wouldn't give to walk away from all of this. I don't know if I can wait."

"Maybe you don't have to." He leaned over her. The windows of his black SUV were tinted. No one was around to notice when he slid a hand beneath her skirt and ran his fingers from her ankle up her thigh to the edge of her satiny underpants.

"Um, Hutch…" She gripped the door handle with her right hand.

"Relax, Simone."

That was easy for him to say. Her entire body clenched in anticipation of what he was about to do. When he pressed two fingers against the very heart of her yearning, she gasped. Carefully, he pleasured her.

She should have made him stop. Cecelia and Naomi were expecting her inside. But none of that mattered.

Hutch took her somewhere dark and visceral and so compelling, she lost everything except the feel of his hands on her body.

When she came, her fingernails left marks in the leather seat. Chest heaving, she opened one eye. "You're some kind of sorcerer," she said.

His grin was a slash of white teeth beneath his mask. "All the better to seduce you, my dear."

Heart pounding still, she hesitated. This was where her lack of experience failed her. "Do you want me to…"

"No." He said the word forcefully, though his body spoke otherwise. "When I have you in bed tonight, and I'm deep inside you with you crying out my name, *then* I'll get what I'm waiting for…but not before."

Simone nodded, unable to find the words to tell him what she felt. With all her heart, she wanted to believe Hutch would forgive her when she told him the truth. Honestly, she wanted to tell him now and get it over with…end the suspense. That wasn't an option, though. She had a party to execute.

They barely spoke after that. Hutch brooded, gaze trained out his window as Simone fussed with her hair and makeup. When she was reasonably certain she was back to normal, she picked up her small clutch purse. "I'm ready."

The Bellamy was magnificent. From the vast, sophisticated lobby, down the wide hallways covered in luxurious Oriental rugs, to the entranceway into the ballroom, the place was awash in flowers and tiny white lights and golden gauze bows. Pale orchids in cream and lavender emitted a subtle fragrance. Cecelia's touch was on every bit of design and decor in the building. This new hotel was destined to become a centerpiece of Royal's social scene.

Hutch was deeply grateful he was wearing a mask. He felt raw and gutted. If he hadn't known he was in love with Simone before, he knew it tonight. She was incandescent. Pregnancy gave her a glow of contentment. His physical need for her was only outweighed by a gut-deep certainty that she was the only woman who could make him whole.

After his stunt in the car, which slowed Simone and him down, a crowd of guests already gathered in the lobby and moved toward the ballroom.

The Bellamy had hired ample staff for the big evening. In addition to its own roster of chefs and waiters, tonight's event demanded even more. Every guest would be expecting perfection.

Even with attendees wearing masks, it was easy to pick out a few here and there. He was almost certain he identified Harper Lake with one of the Tate brothers, though he couldn't tell the twins apart. Clay Everett limped in with his gorgeous secretary. That might raise a few eyebrows.

Thirty minutes after the official starting time of the masquerade ball, the room was packed. Old friends and new. Octogenarians whose history went way back in Royal. Young, hip entrepreneurs who had made their mark in reshaping the town. Everything in between.

After twenty minutes of mingling and chatting, Simone was flushed and sparkling with excitement. "Let's dance," she said.

"I thought you'd never ask."

Hutch led her onto the floor and tucked her against his chest. With Simone wearing heels, they could have kissed easily. He inhaled sharply, dizzy from the scent of delicate perfume and warm female skin.

He held her firmly, confidently. As they twirled around the room, he saw people watching them. All male eyes were on Simone. She would stand out in any crowd with her dark hair and sexy dress. His arms tightened around her. No man in the room was good enough for her, not even him.

Over the past few weeks, Simone had told him stories about the headaches involved in planning tonight's event. The committee had squabbled over which band to hire. A few people wanted a modern, trendy group. But in the end, given the stately atmosphere of the hotel and the knowledge that the crowd would include a variety of ages, the decision was made to go with a small orchestra. The playlist included songs from all decades, primarily the kind of romantic pieces that encouraged slow dancing cheek to cheek.

Hutch thought it was a brilliant strategy. When a man dressed up in a monkey suit and took a woman out on the town, he wanted to be able to hold her. Vertical foreplay. That's what it was. And he couldn't wait to get Simone horizontal.

Occasionally, the band would break into a fast, snappy number so the folks who really knew how to dance had a chance to shine out on the floor. Simone was a good dancer, and Hutch was decent…but she begged off because of the babies. Her lengthy illness had sapped her stamina. Now she appeared to be slowing down. Instinctively, he wrapped his arms around her.

"I'm dying of thirst," she said, leaning into him. "And I wouldn't mind sampling that menu I've spent weeks planning."

Sixteen

Hutch steered a path to the buffet with Simone in tow. The spread was amazing, even by Royal's standards. Prime rib, of course. After all, this was cattle country. But also chicken kebabs skewered with vegetables, crab puffs and enormous prawns iced down in a magnificent crystal bowl. Not to mention all the usual accoutrements.

"Well," he said. "Anything you want me to avoid?" He was keenly aware that even the sight of certain foods was enough to set off Simone's nausea. This was her special night. He didn't want to take any chances.

She leaned her head against his shoulder momentarily. "That's sweet of you, Hutch. I think I'm okay, though. I won't attempt the caviar, but everything else looks good to me right now."

They filled their plates to overflowing and sought

out a table for two in a distant corner. Large potted plants provided cover for discreet trysts. "Was this your idea?" he asked as he held out her chair and helped her get seated. They were sheltered, although not completely private, of course.

She popped a carrot stick in her mouth and grinned. "Romance is alive and well in Royal...didn't you know?"

"I'll grab us a couple of drinks."

"Plain tap water, please."

When he returned moments later, Simone sat with her chin on her hand staring at a large stuffed mushroom with a frown. He handed a glass. "What's wrong?"

She shrugged. "I don't know about this one."

"Then for God's sake, don't take any chances," he said. He filched the mushroom and popped it into his mouth. Fortunately, the rest of her choices were winners.

The food was excellent, but he knew he was in trouble when just watching her eat made him hard again. Soft lips. Small white teeth. Lord help him. Simone was oblivious to his mood, her gaze tracking various couples on the dance floor. She named them off one by one.

"How do you do that?" he asked. "Isn't the whole point of a masquerade ball anonymity? I know I've been away a long time, but I only managed to spot a few people I could identify for sure."

"I cheated," she confessed. "I was the one who processed all the names and built the spreadsheet. Even with everyone wearing masks, I think I could name most of them."

"My hat's off to you. I'm guessing a few of those couples who responded were a surprise?"

"Oh, yes. Definitely. I *would* tell you, but then I'd have to kill you."

"Isn't that taking secret identities a step too far, Mata Hari?"

"You could always try to torture it out of me."

Her big blue eyes were wide and innocent. When she stuck out her tongue to catch a bit of cocktail sauce at the corner of her mouth, he sighed. "You're messing with me, aren't you?"

"Would *I* do that?"

"In a heartbeat."

He reached across the table and took her hands in his. "You think you're safe from retaliation because we're in a public place, but fair warning, my sweet. I could toss you over my shoulder, walk out of here to the front desk and get a room."

"You wouldn't…" She eyed him askance.

"Try me."

"Okay, Hutch," she said, her tone placating. "I'll behave from here on out. No flirting. No innuendo. No dancing."

"I didn't say no dancing. A man has to take what crumbs he can get."

She cocked her head. "I'm confused. Are you a barbarian laying down the law or a puppy begging for scraps?"

He stroked the backs of her hands with his thumbs. "What do you think?"

For a long second, their gazes locked. Her eyes were nothing so simple as blue. They were dark at the outer rim, like midnight, but lighter near the pupil. He was mesmerized studying them.

"Hutch?"

He heard her say his name, but he was lost in a fantasy where she was stark naked on his bed. "Hmm?"

"We probably should get back out there since we've finished eating. After all, I'm one of the ones in charge."

"Yes…" He whispered the word, still caught up in a vision he hoped like hell would come true in only a few hours.

Suddenly, his dream woman stood up. "Hurry," she said, excitement in her voice. "I think Deacon is about to make an announcement."

Hutch followed her, disgruntled. They found a spot near the front. The stage was set up just behind the orchestra. Deacon Chase stood at the microphone with a genial smile on his face and a raised hand. When the crowd at last fell silent, he spoke.

"First of all, friends and neighbors, Shane Delgado and I would like to welcome you to The Bellamy. This hotel and all it encompasses is a dream come true for us. We're delighted to have all of you here tonight. I hope you'll spend a lot of time at The Bellamy in the years to come, not only overnight for special occasions, but also dining with us on a regular basis at either the Silver Saddle or the Glass House. Our new spa, Pure, is open to the public. All you need to do is make a reservation." He paused and cleared his throat. "I know everyone is eager to get back to the dancing, but I hope you'll grant me a moment of personal privilege."

He held out his hand, and to Hutch's surprise, Simone's friend Cecelia took the stage. Deacon introduced her with a broad smile. "If you think we have a beautifully appointed hotel, this is the woman who gets the credit. I'm forever in her debt for helping us make The Bellamy a reality. Even more than that, I am beyond happy that she has agreed to be my wife."

The room erupted in shouts and cheers. Shocked, Hutch looked sideways at Simone. "Did you know about this?"

She nodded, beaming. "He gave her the ring several weeks ago, but they only told close friends and family before tonight. I guess this makes it official. Look how sweet they are together."

He did look, and Simone was right. Judging from the expressions on their faces, Cecelia and Deacon were ridiculously happy with their new status. Hutch continued to brood while Simone joined the crowd of friends who wanted to congratulate the bride-to-be and her groom.

Deacon Chase had chosen well. As far as Hutch could tell, the billionaire hotelier and the gorgeous platinum blonde had a lot in common. Case in point— the two of them, along with Delgado, had turned a dream into a reality. Deacon built hotels. Cecelia had the know-how to furnish them.

What did Hutch and Simone have in common? Not one damn thing.

Suddenly, his bow tie choked him, and the room was far too hot. His heart beat out an unfamiliar cadence in his chest. Working his way over to Simone, he reached out and tapped her on the arm. The crowd was so noisy, he had to bend down so she could hear him.

"I'm going outside for some fresh air," he said. "Stay here and enjoy your friends."

Big blue eyes searched his face. "Are you okay?"

He dredged up a smile and brushed the back of his

hand across her cheek. "Never better," he lied. "I'll be back shortly."

"How will you find me?"

Was she serious? "Honey, that red dress stands out in a crowd. Don't worry. I won't leave without you."

Desperately, he plowed his way to the other side of the room. Had the fire marshal okayed this crowd? Hell, the marshal had probably been invited for that very reason.

Outside, he jerked his bow tie off and stuffed it in his pocket. After that, he took a deep, cleansing breath and leaned against a marble statue of Pan in a clump of daisies. He wished he smoked. Since he didn't and never had, the next best thing was walking. He'd read the press packet about the new hotel. The grounds included several miles of wooded trails.

He didn't care where he went at this point. It wasn't like he could get lost. This was Royal, not the middle of a wilderness.

The night was perfect…too perfect. He walked with his head down, trying not to notice the moonlight or the sweet scent of flowers in the air. If he proposed to Simone and she accepted, there would be no going back. He wouldn't be able to return to Sudan to escape her hold on him.

Could he and would he be able to love three babies who weren't his biological offspring? That seemed the least of his worries at this point. He adored children. He always had. Besides, the triplets carried half of their mother's DNA. If he loved Simone, he would love her babies, too.

But what if he proposed and she said no? Why had he purchased a house so near hers? He had to drive by Simone's house every day on the way to work. That would be unbearable if they broke up for a second time.

He'd never been good at games of chance. Knowing the odds were stacked against him meant he'd never had any real trouble staying away from gambling. He liked being in control.

Yet here he was, contemplating a course that was neither certain nor even advisable. On paper it seemed absurd. His parents clearly agreed. Why would he risk so much when he had no idea if Simone cared for him at all?

Again, he visited the possibility that she was using him. With triplets on the way, she might think she needed a second parent in the house above all else. Such a rationale made her seem cold and calculating. The Simone he knew was neither of those things.

When he regained a modicum of control over his emotions, he put on the bow tie again. It was time for him to go back inside to smile and to dance and to do whatever it took to make it through the remainder of the ball. After that, he'd get his reward. One whole night in Simone's bed. Or his. He wasn't too picky about locale.

As he turned around to head back the way he had come, a large man about Hutch's height stepped out of the shadows and blocked the path. Hutch froze, sensing danger. But the man was in formal attire and wore one of the masquerade masks. Surely this wasn't some gate-crasher come late to wreck the party.

"What can I do for you, sir?"

The man straightened. He was big and broad, but even in the moonlight Hutch could see that his face was gaunt. "It's what I can do for you, Dr. Hutchinson."

"Who are you? How do you know my name?"

"You can call me Maverick. It doesn't matter how I know your name. I'm here to give you fair warning about the woman in the red dress."

Hutch frowned. "Simone?"

"Of course, Simone. Who else? You don't have a clue what she's really up to, do you?"

"This conversation is over." Hutch was furious and perturbed underneath that. Why did the stranger even care? Hutch went to brush past him, but the old guy put a beefy hand smack in the middle of Hutch's chest. "Don't run off, young man. I'm here to save you from yourself."

"It sounds to me like you're here to bad-mouth Simone. And I don't care to listen anymore."

The man got up in his face. "That little slut in the red dress got pregnant on purpose so she could inherit half of her grandfather's estate. Did your precious Simone ever bother to tell you *that* twist in the story?"

"You're lying," Hutch said. Fury blurred his vision. He wanted to drag the man into the moonlight and see his face. With the mask and the shadows, he hadn't a clue who he was.

"It's no lie. You ask her. And ask her if she knows Maverick. I think you'll be unpleasantly surprised."

"Go to hell." Hutch shoved past him, determined to walk away without indulging in a fistfight. He knew how to fell an assailant, but he'd rather not in this setting.

The other man was older, but bulkier. Hutch never even saw the blow coming. It caught him in the tem-

ple. Something sharp, a ring perhaps, cut into his skin.
Then he fell hard and hit his head.

Simone began to worry when Hutch didn't come
back after half an hour. Fifteen minutes after that she
decided to go in search of him. She didn't bother with
looking inside the hotel. He had professed a need for
fresh air.

Outside, she inhaled deeply, happy to be away from
the crush of the party. It was, by every measure, a
grand success. She and Naomi and Cecelia could be
justifiably proud of what they had managed to pull
off. The money raised for Homes and Hearts would be
enough to build modest homes for three needy families.

Even knowing that her event was a smashing victory wasn't enough to erase her unease. She walked
away from the building toward the parking area.
"Hutch!" she called out, her voice fraught with worry.
She noticed that the space in and around the cars had
been landscaped beautifully. Plenty of places to hide
if a person or a couple didn't want to be discovered.

"Hutch!" She stood by his car now, only a little relieved to see it was still there. At least he hadn't left
the premises.

Still no answer. She followed a series of small sign-
posts leading back into the trees. For a moment, she
stood, irresolute. Normally, she would take more care
with her personal safety. This was private property,
though. She had seen at least a dozen uniformed secu-
rity guards mingling with the crowd and monitoring
the entrances and exits. No one was out here trying
to mug unwary party guests.

At least she hoped not.

She continued to walk, half a mile at least. Her shoes were not meant for traipsing about in the woods. When the pain of a blister became too much to handle, she stopped and took off her expensive footwear. Chances were, the heels were a loss. When she looked back, she could see the hotel in the distance all lit up like a fairy-tale castle. "Hutch!"

A faint groan was her only answer. She almost tripped over him. "Hutch!" She knelt urgently, reassured in part when she heard him breathing. "Hutch, it's Simone. Wake up." Frustrated and scared, she removed his mask and her own. This was no time for pretense.

She had no water, no rag to put water *on*. No way to sponge his face and wake him up. Nevertheless, she got one arm around his shoulders and held him against her breast. "Hutch. Can you hear me? It's Simone. What happened to you?" Even in the shadowy woods, she could see something dark against his temple. When she tested it with a fingertip, she got woozy. Blood. Definitely blood.

Gently, she ran her fingers over his scalp and discovered a second injury, this one an enormous knot. He must have hit his head when he fell. But that didn't explain the wound at his temple.

Why hadn't she brought someone with her? This was the worst rescue attempt in the history of rescue attempts. She wished she remembered her first-aid training.

It seemed as if she held him forever, but in reality only five or ten minutes elapsed. She stroked his forehead carefully, speaking to him in a jumble of whispered words. Fear unlike any she had ever known paralyzed her. She couldn't lose Hutch. Not again. Not forever.

Part of her wanted to run for help. The other part was desperately afraid to leave him here alone in the dark. So she stayed…and she prayed.

At last, Hutch regained consciousness. Slowly, he stirred. She felt him stiffen as he realized where he was. With her help, he sat all the way up, putting his head in his hands, groaning and cursing beneath his breath.

"Tell me how this happened," she pleaded. "Who did this to you?"

"Would you believe I ran into a door?"

"That's not funny. Let me help you up."

He batted her hand away. "I can do it."

It took him two tries, but he managed. His truculent independence was a good thing, because Simone had no idea how she would have managed to stand with a two-hundred-pound man draped across her shoulder.

When he swayed, she reached for him. Again, he eluded her touch. Instead, he leaned on the nearest tree.

"Are you able to walk?" she asked calmly. Something bad had happened. She knew it in her gut. Something beyond Hutch's head wounds. His body language screamed at her to stay away.

He nodded. "I can do it."

They were farther from the hotel than Simone first realized. Hutch made it a quarter of a mile or so before he had to sit down and rest.

"This is stupid," she said. "You stay here. I'll go get help."

"No!" He shouted the word and then cursed again as his outburst clearly caused him agony.

"You might have a concussion."

"I'm a doctor. I don't need *you* to practice medicine."

Now she was certain something was wrong. The disdain in his voice, edged with fury, was a far cry from the Hutch who had wanted to make love to her in a tucked-away corner.

Her heart sank. She waited in silence until he was able to stand again. This time she knew better than to offer help.

They made it only as far as the parking lot. Beneath a streetlight, she caught her first glimpse of the wound at his temple. It was an angry red knot, sliced clean through with a cut that oozed significant amounts of blood.

"Tell me what happened, Hutch. Who did this to you?"

He leaned against his own vehicle. She saw his chest rise and fall as he struggled to speak. "Does the name Maverick mean anything to you, Simone?"

Seventeen

Dread made her blood run cold. Her voice froze in her throat.

Hutch's gaze was bitter. "I see that it does. Your face gives you away."

Hot tears burned her eyes, but she didn't let them fall. "Maverick is the stranger who has been sending mysterious, threatening messages to people in Royal. I got two of his nasty notes, but so have others."

"I don't really care about anyone else but you, Simone. Why would an anonymous blackmailer have anything to hold over *your* head?" The words were icy and clipped. It appeared that Hutch was prepared to be judge and jury.

"How do you even know about this?"

Hutch shrugged, wincing as he did so. "I ran into him on the trail. He confronted me. We argued. I tried to leave. He punched me."

"You need X-rays, Hutch. Please go to the hospital."

"First things first, Simone. Tell me... Is it fair to say that you got pregnant only to satisfy the terms of your grandfather's will?"

Hutch watched her face. Every drop of color washed away. Her eyes welled with tears. He had his answer. "My God," he said. "It's true." His heart shattered into sharp pieces that stabbed his chest. "You wanted money, so you decided to have a baby. Do you have any idea how incredibly selfish and immoral that is? I've spent my entire career protecting mothers and babies. What you did is unconscionable."

She stood proud and tall as he annihilated her. "I made a foolish mistake. I admit that. But it wasn't really about the money, I swear."

"Of course it wasn't," he sneered.

"I'm telling you the truth," she cried. "Let's go back inside so you can sit down. I'll explain everything."

He shook his head violently, almost welcoming the pain. "I don't need to hear your explanations. I see it all now. That's the real reason you sent me off to Africa, isn't it, Simone? You thought you were dating an up-and-coming surgeon, but then you found out I was more interested in offering my services to the poor than building a mansion in Royal and inviting you to be lady of the manor."

"Tonight isn't a good time to discuss this," she said quietly. "Come back inside with me. I'll get some ice for your head."

When she tried to take his arm, he jerked away. He saw the agony in her eyes, but he didn't care. He didn't care about anything at this moment. "I'm sure there are a number of people at the ball who will be glad to take you home, Simone. You and I are done here. In fact, we're done permanently."

"Hutch, please..." Tears spilled down her cheeks. "You're twisting the facts and coming up with the wrong answers. This isn't as bad as it seems."

He opened the car door and managed not to groan when he slid behind the wheel. "I don't want to hear it, Simone. Goodbye." Barely allowing her time to jump out of the way, he put the car in gear and screeched out of the parking lot. Though he was cautious getting out of town, when he made it to the interstate, he pressed down on the accelerator and tried to outrun his demons.

Thank God he hadn't told her he loved her. That would have been the final indignity. He felt like a credulous fool. Hell, he *was* a fool. He had let hot sex blind him to Simone's real nature. She was a user and a manipulator.

He drove on into the night with no particular destination in mind. At last, though, his massive headache forced him to pull off and find a motel room for the night. The clerk gaped at him—he must have looked like something out of a horror movie—but handed over the key without protest.

Hutch parked in front of the door to 11C. He had no suitcase, no shaving kit, nothing. What did it matter?

Before he could collapse onto the bed, he had one phone call to make. He was scheduled to work Saturday and Sunday. Fortunately, he was able to get in touch with his second in command, who agreed to switch shifts for a couple of days.

That left Hutch totally unencumbered for the next

forty-eight hours. He stumbled into the bathroom, took a quick shower and carefully washed the wound on his head. Then he went back into the other room, pulled back the hideous bedspread and fell facedown on the mattress.

The following morning, he awoke with the hangover from hell. Then he realized he hadn't been drinking. After that, he remembered that Simone was gone. He felt empty inside. Though he was hungry, no amount of food could fix what was wrong with him.

Even so, he couldn't sit around in his tux all weekend. He downed some acetaminophen and made it out to the car on shaky legs. Fortunately, there was a diner nearby…the ubiquitous staple of rural Texas. The waitress took one look at his face and didn't bother with chitchat.

After a hearty meal of bacon, eggs and toast, Hutch felt marginally better. Next on his list was a stop at a discount store. There he found a pair of jeans that fit his long, lanky body. He grabbed a couple of plain knit shirts, some underwear and socks, and cheap sneakers.

Back at the motel, he took another shower. It was hot as hell outside. Afterward, he put on his new duds and stretched out on the bed to watch TV. He rarely had time in his life for something so mindless and sedentary. Every day was filled with work and more work and, recently, Simone.

For the first time, he allowed himself to remember what had happened. There was plenty to be pissed about. The worst was that she had lied to him. By omission, but still. She told him she got pregnant because she wanted to be a mother.

Maybe that part was true, but it wasn't the whole truth. The real truth was money. Lots of it. People would do almost anything for money.

Eventually, his anger was replaced by a dull acceptance. Maybe he wasn't supposed to get married and have a family of his own. Maybe he was supposed to devote his life to helping other people have healthy babies.

By Sunday morning, both bumps on his head were healing nicely. In addition to his new clothes, he had bought a handheld mirror so he could look at the knot on the back of his skull. That was a mistake, because suddenly the memory of Simone stroking his brow and running her fingers over his head came back with a vengeance.

He had to check out of the room by eleven. After that task was accomplished, he sat in his car and clenched the steering wheel with two hands. One thing was certain. He was not returning to Royal in order to worm his way back into Simone's good graces. He probably wasn't even in love with her, not really. He'd been dazzled by good sex and his need to watch over triplets who needed him.

Slowly, he cruised the small town, which was little more than a wide space in the road. They had a fast-food place but little else. The only meal he had eaten was breakfast yesterday. His stomach had been rolling and pitching too much to think about food again. Now, though, he was hungry.

In the drive-through he ordered a double cheeseburger with fries and a Coke. His whole life was in ruins. Why not indulge in junk food, as well?

The calorie-laden meal filled the hole in his stomach. Unfortunately, the aching maw in his chest was not so easily appeased. It hurt. His whole body hurt. So be it.

He turned the vehicle around and headed for Royal. Monday morning would come bright and early. He'd taken far too much advantage of his flexible schedule lately. If he kept this up, the hospital board would decide they had made a mistake in hiring him.

Hutch was good at medicine. He was lousy at love. It made sense to concentrate on the one aspect of his life that had never disappointed him.

When he finally made it back to Royal, darkness had fallen. He deliberately avoided looking at Simone's house when he was forced to pass by it on the way to his. At home, he walked from room to room, pacing aimlessly. In the back bedroom there were still a few boxes he hadn't unpacked yet. Maybe he would list the place this week and move across town.

If he were honest, though, he didn't want to give Simone the satisfaction of knowing she had that kind of power over him. He'd been taken in by a pro, but he didn't have to let it happen again.

Monday morning, he showed up for work clean shaven and bright eyed. He'd slept reasonably well from sheer exhaustion. Despite that, the pain in his chest and his gut remained. Doggedly, he concentrated on the cases at hand. His own personal trauma would not be allowed to interfere with the quality of his performance.

The day lasted a thousand hours. It was all he could do to dispel the images of Simone from his mind. She was what she was. He needed to cut his losses and move on.

He was thirty minutes from finishing his shift when he ran into Janine.

She frowned at him. "You look like hell. Are you ill? Go home, Hutch. Get some rest."

"I'm not sick," he said. "Just tired. I was about to leave."

"I know you're glad Simone is doing better," she said.

Hutch went still. "Oh?"

Janine frowned. "I assumed you've been with her since she got out of the hospital. Isn't that why you look like you're running on four hours' sleep?"

"I haven't seen Simone recently," he said carefully. "What's wrong with her?"

The other doctor stared at him. "She collapsed at the party Friday night. One of the guests found her in the parking lot. No one could find you, so they called an ambulance."

Hutch felt his bones turn to water. "An ambulance?"

"Her blood pressure skyrocketed. She had some kind of panic attack. Because she was already weak from the battle with nausea, we had to give her IV fluids again. Simone told me you were meeting her at her house. That was the only reason I released her when I did."

"I wasn't there," Hutch said slowly. His heart slugged in his chest. "But I'm headed there now. Thank you, Janine."

This couldn't be happening again. Another woman he cared about slipping away, and him powerless to save her. Simone wasn't perfect. If he took a mental step backward, though, he could admit that the love she had demonstrated for her babies was real and fierce.

Maybe he had made too much of her original motives. God knows, he had screwed up at several major points in his own life. Was it fair to judge Simone for *her* missteps, when his had been equally egregious?

The truth dawned slowly, in tandem with incredulity. The reason he'd been so angry with her at the party was because he loved her. Her betrayal had cut straight through to his heart, leaving him bleeding in more ways than one.

He drove like a madman, half expecting to find Simone unconscious or worse. When she answered the door at his first knock, the moment was anticlimactic at best.

"Why did you lie to your doctor?" he demanded, going on the attack.

Simone gazed at him with blank eyes. "What are you doing here, Hutch?" She didn't back up, and she sure as hell didn't invite him in.

Suddenly, everything coalesced into one shining bubble of certainty. "We need to talk." He said the words quietly, trying not to spook her.

"I don't think so." She tried to shut the door, but he stuck his foot in the opening.

"Please, Simone. Let me speak my piece. Then if you want, I'll leave."

She lifted one shoulder in a careless shrug. "Whatever."

He closed the door behind him and followed her to the den. Simone chose a straight-back chair. Hutch decided to stand. "I'm in love with you," he said bluntly.

Her eyelids flickered, but the look on her face didn't change. "I see."

"I don't care if those babies aren't my biological children. I want to be their daddy."

"That's not going to happen." At last a spark of blue in those lovely eyes gave him hope. He couldn't get through to frozen Simone. Angry Simone was another story.

He ran a hand over the back of his neck. "I've done a lot of thinking in the last seventy-two hours. I was a fool to think your motives for carrying those babies were anything but pure. It was a knee-jerk reaction. You'll never know how sorry I am for not trusting you."

"And that's supposed to make me feel better? You shut me out, Hutch, and not for the first time." Her anger made him wince.

"I know. My only excuse is that your Maverick guy got inside my head. As far as your inheritance goes, who am I to judge? Money isn't a bad thing in and of itself."

"Just people like me…" Her facade cracked. For a moment, he saw how deeply he had hurt her.

"Oh, God, Simone." He knelt at her feet. "I was an ass. I lost you once. I won't lose you again. I love you, and I'm pretty sure you love me, too. Marry me, sweetheart. Let's make a family together. Forgive me, little mama."

She lifted a hand to touch the scab at his temple. "People would talk."

"Let them. Nothing matters except you and me and those precious babies. I won't give up on us. I won't. This is too important."

Simone eluded his hold and stood, fleeing to the other side of the room. She had her back to him, so he couldn't read her expression. "There's something else you should know," she said.

His chest tightened. "Oh?"

After a long silence, she turned around. "You wouldn't be marrying an heiress."

"I don't understand."

"As soon as I deliver these babies, I receive five million dollars. That was the deal. I could only inherit my share of the estate if I produced an heir of my own. Otherwise, all of it went to my father. But my lawyer has drawn up papers to put three million in trust, one million for each of the children when they turn twenty-five."

"Two million is still a lot of money."

"That's how much I'm donating to Homes and Hearts. I didn't want to keep any of it. Not after the way you looked at me Friday night. I need you to understand why I did what I did."

"You don't have to explain. You're entitled to your own choices."

Her short laugh held little humor. "Don't you mean my own mistakes? Here's the thing, Hutch. I've been jockeying for my father's attention my whole life. He and my grandfather made no secret of the fact that I was a disappointment. They wanted a boy, another Parker male to carry on the family tradition. When I heard the terms of the will, I was hurt. And angry. I've never been good enough, you know?"

"Simone—"

She held up a hand, cutting him short. "I don't want you feeling sorry for me. It is what it is. But I'm keeping the land. Those acres of Texas are my birthright. Generations of Parkers have lived there and ranched and farmed and done whatever they had to do to survive. I won't apologize for wanting that legacy, not only for me, but for my children."

He exhaled, his shoulders tight. "Are you done?"

"What else is there to say?"

"You could tell me you love me." He managed to say the words jokingly, but the fear he had ruined something precious choked him. Simone's silence was frankly terrifying. "I'll grovel if need be, my sweet firecracker."

He saw the muscles in her throat work as she swallowed. "You'll want children of your own."

It wasn't a question. He frowned. "I think it would be more correct to say I will want *more* children of my own. I already cherish those three little lives you're carrying. I don't care if their biological father is blond and blue-eyed. We live in a global world. I grew up understanding that many people drew lines to shut me out. I want to make a family with you, of children who never have to know those limits. We'll build our lives around love, Simone. You and I were both made to feel less at times, but that's over. Tell me you believe that. Tell me you love me. Tell me I didn't destroy our second chance."

His life hung in the balance.

Tears rolled down cheeks that were too pale. She came to him at last, sliding her arms around his waist and resting her cheek over his heart. "I do love you, Hutch. I never stopped. And, yes…I want to marry you and make a family together."

"Thank God." He held her tightly, his own eyes damp. "I adore you. I swear you won't regret this."

After long, aching moments, Simone pulled back and looked up at him. "I'm sorry these babies aren't yours," she said, regret shadowing her gaze. "I'm so very sorry."

He shook his head, feeling everything in his world settle into his place. "That's where you're wrong, my love. Those babies *are* mine, in every way that counts. I love them, and I love you. Now hush, and let me kiss you."

Simone smiled at him tremulously. "Only a kiss?"

"Oh, no," he said, scooping her into his arms. "We have a lot of makeup sex coming our way."

His bride-to-be gave him a wicked grin, looking more like herself at last. "Then let's get started, Dr. Hutchinson. I've been waiting a long time for this."

He strode down the hall and up the stairs with his precious burden. "So have I, sweet Simone. So have I…"

* * * * *

* * *

If you're on Twitter, tell us what you think of
Harlequin Desire! #harlequindesire

COMING NEXT MONTH FROM

Available July 3, 2017

#2527 THE BABY FAVOR
Billionaires and Babies • by Andrea Laurence
CEO Mason Spencer and his wife are headed for divorce when an old
promise changes their plans. They are now the guardians for Spencer's
niece...and they must remain married. Will this be their second chance,
one that leads to forever?

#2528 LONE STAR BABY SCANDAL
Texas Cattleman's Club: Blackmail • by Lauren Canan
When sexy former rodeo champion turned billionaire Clay Everett sets his
sights on his spunky secretary, he's sure he holds the reins in their affair.
Until he learns Sophie Prescott is carrying his child. Now all bets are off!

#2529 HIS UNEXPECTED HEIR
Little Secrets • by Maureen Child
After a fling with a sexy marine leaves Rita pregnant, her attempts to reach
the billionaire are met with silence...until now! Brooding, reclusive Jack
offers to marry Rita—in name only. Will his new family give him the heart to
embrace life—and love—again?

#2530 PREGNANT BY THE BILLIONAIRE
The Locke Legacy • by Karen Booth
Billionaire Sawyer Locke only makes commitments to his hotel empire—
until he meets fiery PR exec Kendall Ross. Now he can't get her out of his
mind—or out of his bed. But when she becomes pregnant, will he claim
the heir he never expected?

#2531 BEST FRIEND BRIDE
In Name Only • by Kat Cantrell
CEO Jonas Kim must stop his arranged marriage—by arranging a marriage
for himself! His best friend, Vivian, will be his wife and never fall in love, or
so he thinks. Can he keep his heart safe when Viv tempts him to become
friends with benefits?

#2532 CLAIMING THE COWGIRL'S BABY
Red Dirt Royalty • by Silver James
Rancher Kaden inherited a birth father, a powerful last name and wealth—
none of which he wants. His pregnant lover, debutante Pippa Duncan, has
lost everything due to a dark family secret. Their marriage of convenience
may undo the pain of their families' pasts, but will it lead to love?

**YOU CAN FIND MORE INFORMATION ON UPCOMING HARLEQUIN® TITLES,
FREE EXCERPTS AND MORE AT WWW.HARLEQUIN.COM.**

HDCNM0617

SPECIAL EXCERPT FROM

H HARLEQUIN®

Desire

*When billionaire boss Cameron McNeill goes
undercover in a tropical paradise to check out his
newest hotel's employees, he doesn't expect to want to
claim beautiful concierge Maresa Delphine and her
surprise baby as his own...*

Read on for a sneak peek at
HIS ACCIDENTAL HEIR
by Joanne Rock

As soon as he banished the hotel staff, including Maresa
Delphine, he'd find a quiet spot on the beach where he
could recharge.

Maresa punched a button on the guest elevator while
a young man disappeared down another hall with the
luggage. Cameron's gaze settled on the bare arch of her
neck just above her jacket collar. Her thick brown hair
had been clipped at the nape, ending in a silky tail that
curled along one shoulder. A single pearl drop earring
was a pale contrast to the rich brown of her skin.

She glanced up at him. Caught him staring.

The jolt of awareness flared hot and unmistakable. He
could tell she felt it, too. Her pupils dilated a fraction,
dark pools with golden rims. His heartbeat slugged
heavier. Harder.

He forced his gaze away as the elevator chimed to
announce their arrival on his floor. "After you."

He held the door as she stepped out into the short hall. Cameron used the key card to unlock the suite, not sure what to expect. So far, Maresa had proven a worthy concierge. That was good for the hotel. Less favorable for him, perhaps, since her high standards surely precluded acting on a fleeting elevator attraction.

"If everything is to your satisfaction, Mr. Holmes, I'll leave you undisturbed while I go make your dinner reservations for the week." She hadn't even allowed the door to close behind them, a wise practice, of course, for a female hotel employee.

The young man he'd seen earlier was already in the hall behind her with the luggage cart. Cameron could hear her giving the bellhop instructions.

"Thank you." Cameron turned his back on her to stare out at the view of the hotel's private beach and the brilliant turquoise Caribbean Sea. "For now, I'm satisfied."

The room, of course, was fine. Ms. Delphine had passed his first test.

But satisfied? No.

He wouldn't rest until he knew why the guest reviews of the Carib Grand Hotel were less positive than anticipated. And satisfaction was the last thing he was feeling when the most enticing woman he'd met in a long time was off-limits.

That attraction would be difficult to ignore when it was imperative he uncover all her secrets.

Don't miss
HIS ACCIDENTAL HEIR by Joanne Rock,
available June 2017 wherever
Harlequin® Desire books and ebooks are sold.

www.Harlequin.com

Love the Harlequin book you just read?

Your opinion matters.

Review this book on your favorite
book site, review site, blog or your own
social media properties and share
your opinion with other readers!

Be sure to connect with us at:
Harlequin.com/Newsletters
Facebook.com/HarlequinBooks
Twitter.com/HarlequinBooks

Whatever You're Into... Passionate Reads

Looking for more passionate reads from Harlequin®?
Fear not! Harlequin® Presents, Harlequin® Desire and
Harlequin® Blaze offer you irresistible romance stories
featuring powerful heroes.

♦HARLEQUIN *Presents.*

Do you want alpha males, decadent glamour and jet-set
lifestyles? Step into the sensational, sophisticated world of
Harlequin® Presents, where sinfully tempting heroes ignite a
fierce and wickedly irresistible passion!

♦HARLEQUIN *Desire*

Harlequin® Desire novels are powerful, passionate and
provocative contemporary romances set against a backdrop of
wealth, privilege and sweeping family saga. Alpha heroes with
a soft side meet strong-willed but vulnerable heroines amid a
dramatic world of divided loyalties, high-stakes conflict and
intense emotion.

♦HARLEQUIN *Blaze*

Harlequin® Blaze stories sizzle with strong heroines and
irresistible heroes playing the game of modern love and lust.
They're fun, sexy and always steamy.

Be sure to check out our full selection of books
within each series every month!

www.Harlequin.com

HPASSION2016